MODERN

Glamour. Power. Passion.

MILLS & BOON

First Published 2025
First Australian Paperback Edition 2025
ISBN 978 1 038 94044 5

ITALIAN'S PREGNANT MISTRESS © 2025 by Carol Marinellli
Philippine Copyright 2025
Australian Copyright 2025
New Zealand Copyright 2025

Published by
Harlequin Mills & Boon
An imprint of Harlequin Enterprises (Australia) Pty Limited
(ABN 47 001 180 918), a subsidiary of HarperCollins
Publishers Australia Pty Limited
(ABN 36 009 913 517)
Level 19, 201 Elizabeth Street
SYDNEY NSW 2000 AUSTRALIA

MIX
Paper | Supporting
responsible forestry
FSC® C001695
www.fsc.org

Italian's Pregnant Mistress

Carol Marinelli

MILLS & BOON

Carol Marinelli recently filled in a form asking for her job title. Thrilled to be able to put down her answer, she put "writer." Then it asked what Carol did for relaxation and she put down the truth—"writing." The third question asked for her hobbies. Well, not wanting to look obsessed, she crossed her fingers and answered "swimming"—but, given that the chlorine in the pool does terrible things to her highlights, I'm sure you can guess the real answer!

Dear Sister Anne,
Love always
Sister Carol

PROLOGUE

A NEW YEAR.

Professionally, Dante Casadio had no resolutions.

He was at the top of his game.

And while the skies might be raining sleet, in the board-room of a top Milan legal firm people were loosening ties and sipping water as things heated up.

Dante's silk tie remained beautifully knotted, his glass untouched.

It was the end of the second week after the Christmas break—and apart from a brief trip to Lucca he had been in his office most days.

The New Year had started as the last had ended—with his exceptionally famous client insisting, 'She can't do this!'

'Nobody is doing anything,' Dante responded in rich Italian. 'It's an extremely reasonable offer.'

'We'll let the judge decide.'

Vincenzo, his senior paralegal, cast Dante a worried glance.

'I mean it,' the client insisted. 'I'll see her in court!' he continued angrily, but Dante said nothing.

Emotional outbursts didn't faze him.

In any capacity.

Be it at work with an overwrought client, or at decadent play with a beautiful lover, his impenetrable barrier was maintained.

Always.

If anything, he found such displays mildly interesting. Possibly because he allowed for so few emotions of his own.

Certainly he never shared how he was feeling with another.

The client, though, was more than ready to share his!

And, rather loudly, he did.

Dante's haughty face remained impassive throughout the rant, and finally he was winding up.

'No, absolutely not!' the client concluded. 'She's not getting her hands on the chalet in Switzerland. Hell, she doesn't even ski.'

Still Dante said nothing.

'I can't believe you're charging me for this so-called advice...' He sneered and tossed the file towards Dante. 'I thought I was hiring the best in Italy.'

There were many people sitting in the boardroom.

The best of the best.

Attorneys, paralegals, a psychologist, his client's PR, as well as his assistant... This eleventh-hour meeting was well attended, by the best of the best, and yet a year on they were getting precisely nowhere.

Dante was rarely wrong—but his client was not concluding his rant. He was escalating.

'I made one mistake!' he shouted. 'One!'

As a colleague tried to defuse the situation with calming words, Dante resisted rolling his eyes.

One mistake?

Please...

As a very sought-after and rather infamous family law attorney, Dante was cynical to the extreme—and he didn't believe a word anyone said. Whether directly, or by omission, Dante knew full well that everyone lied.

Himself included.

But more to the point...

'It's irrelevant,' he said.

His measured, sparse words only further incensed the client, and a vein bulged on his forehead as he refused to accept the fact Dante had calmly delivered—even if his client had strayed, in Italy it was no-fault divorce.

'Legally, your extramarital affair is irrelevant.'

In the heightened emotional world of family law Dante's stony logic was invaluable, and that was why, despite his enormous fees, he was incredibly sought after.

He was not, though, famed for hand-holding.

Dante left that to others.

'You've hired me to deal with financial, property and succession matters. That I can do. However, if you feel you need more time with the practice psychologist...'

'I don't need to see a damn psychologist. I need to speak with my wife.'

'That's the last thing you should do,' Dante warned him sharply. 'The very last thing. Do not contact your soon-to-be *ex*-wife.'

His client sucked in his breath at this reminder of the status of his marriage. 'You're a cold bastard, Casadio.'

Indeed, he was.

As his client thumped the gleaming table Dante Casadio did not flinch.

Vincenzo, his paralegal, was startled, though, and a couple of the other attorneys sat up straighter, perhaps wondering how they would deal with things if this exceptionally high-profile client completely lost his temper.

Rather than clearing the office of staff, or warning the client to calm down, Dante stood up to his well over six-foot height.

There were no signs of confrontation in his stance.

He didn't so much as look at his client.

Nor did he stalk out.

Instead, he picked up the paperwork that was so angrily

being discussed and took a moment to ensure it was in the correct order.

Dante liked order.

His suits were handmade here in Milan. His shoes also. His shirts and ties were from a little further afield—Paris. He liked the cut of a Charvet shirt and remained loyal to them. His thick black hair was trimmed weekly, he shaved daily— even at weekends—and if he was attending a function, as he often did, he shaved twice.

After tapping the paperwork several times on the desk, to ensure it was neatly aligned, he placed it in the rich navy folder.

A tense silence filled the boardroom. All awaited his response, perhaps wondering if he was going to excuse himself from the case…

Of course not.

Dante was more than used to this.

'We shall speak in my office,' he said, and with the file in hand walked to the exit. As he reached the door, he added, 'Immediately.'

He was over the drama—and, as well as that, he had an unexpected phone call to make.

Prior to this meeting Antonia, his PA, had informed him that Sev, his older brother, had called and asked that Dante call him as soon as was convenient.

He and his brother weren't speaking, and the fact that it wasn't Helene, Sev's own PA, who had called had been of instant concern.

'An emergency?' Dante had checked, concerned that something had happened to Gio, their grandfather.

'No.' Antonia had shaken her head. 'But he asked that you call him back today, if possible…'

And he would—just as soon as he had a moment.

Walking into his office, Dante truly wondered how people

could be so attached to *things* that would surely cause nothing but pain.

Aside from a small envelope in his office safe there was nothing he would miss.

Actually, it would be a relief if even that was taken.

Dante had no photos on his desk or shelves, no mementoes. It was the same at his luxurious Milan penthouse, and at his stunning property in Lucca.

Once he had considered the gorgeous Tuscan town home. Now it was a place he avoided until it became...

Unavoidable.

Like at Christmas, or anniversaries.

Why would anyone want constant reminders of anything? Dante thought.

He certainly didn't.

Although he hadn't always been this dispassionate—quite the contrary... As a child he'd been the wild, cheeky one, his charm undeniable, his smile melting hearts...

More so as a teenager and young man.

That smile had won him better favours by then. He'd adored sex and had been passionate lover. A faithful one too—at least for the brief time any tryst had lasted. For he adored women and made it very clear it was just sex...

Good sex.

And lots of it.

With a side serving of charm.

But those days were long gone.

His parents were dead, and he and his brother's once close relationship was severed.

He didn't want to *think* about happier times, let alone feel. And so he didn't.

His relationships were now deliberately remote and brief. He trusted no one and his career was his sole focus.

Dante, despite his client's current anger, knew that come

next Christmas there would be champagne delivered from him and he'd be recommending Dante to colleagues and friends.

Not now, though.

His client stormed in through the door and slammed it closed.

Dante remained seated.

Somehow, despite the status of his client, Dante remained the absolute authority.

Ice versus fire.

And when it came to Dante Casadio ice always won.

Nothing could melt him; his angry client was like a blow torch against a vast glacier...

His client attempted to start where he'd left off, perhaps not understanding that he was in Dante's office now. 'I mean it. She's not getting—'

'Enough!'

Dante called for him to be silent and as the incensed client— angry, offended—met Dante's gaze, no doubt about to remind his attorney of just who he was talking to, the tirade was abruptly halted. There was something in Dante's brown eyes that could, when they so chose, halt an army.

'Take a seat.' Dante gestured to the chair in front of his desk and waited until he had done so. 'If you thump my desk, I shall ask you to leave. If you thump me, I shall see you in criminal court.'

'I just—'

'I've heard enough,' Dante interrupted. He pushed the neat file towards him and stood. 'We can speak again once you have read the proposed settlement in its entirety.'

He walked to the window, staring at the impressive structure of Milan's cathedral.

The documents would take some time to go through, but Dante was used to that.

His intention had never been to specialise in family law, but then, Dante had never lived his life as others intended.

Sev had.

Or rather, he had tried to for a while.

What did his brother want?

God, he hoped Gio was okay.

His grandfather, Gio Casadio, was the only warm place left in Dante's heart—even if he didn't see him that often. He was the only reason he kept a property in Lucca, and his sole reason for returning home.

Even if it killed him to do so.

Dante hated going back...

Their parents had assumed that both the Casadio sons would want to continue on with the lucrative family business in Lucca—a vast winery in the Tuscan hillsides. Yet no one had glimpsed what lay ahead.

At eighteen, when he'd first moved to Milan to study law, Dante's intention had been to focus on corporate law. Sev, the older of the two, had focussed on the hotel industry. Their parents—their father especially—had assumed that their combined skills would progress the business.

Their father had been good at assuming.

No one could have predicted that the once close brothers would fall out on the eve of Sev's wedding.

That Dante, the best man, would be wearing a row of stitches and a black eye almost as dark as his bespoke suit.

Or that the groom's fingers would be too swollen from throwing punches to get his wedding band on.

Not even the sudden and tragic death of their parents and Sev's wife Rosa in a helicopter crash had reunited them.

If anything, the tragedy had driven the brothers further apart.

Oh, they communicated—generally through their personal

assistants—on matters such as the winery, or their grand-father's vast property in Lucca, or his well-being.

The brothers themselves spoke rarely and on a needed basis only.

What did Sev want?

It was then that his client spoke. 'I miss her.'

Dante said nothing, but felt a rare surge of sympathy for his client.

'How we were...'

For a brief second Dante closed his eyes and saw himself and Sev, two little boys running through the vines at home, or playing on the gorgeous walls of Lucca that surrounded the medieval town. They had been so close and, yes, he silently acknowledged, he missed being a brother...

'Listen...' His voice was husky, and he cleared his throat as he snapped his sharp mind back to work. 'Listen to me,' he said in more measured tones as he turned from the window and retook his seat. 'Time is not on your side. Unless you can reach agreement, six weeks from now we go to court and the judge decides. Now.' He put up a hand to stop his client from speaking. 'I don't need to hear about regrets and mistakes or that you miss her. Not in this office. I sort out the finances, the divisions of property, the legalities. I have worked ex-tensively with your wife's attorneys, and this is more than a fair deal. If it goes to litigation, while I shall of course do my best to represent your interests, I don't believe the judge will award you anything close to this.' He gestured to the folder. 'Combine that with my fees and you'll be looking at losing a lot more than a chalet in Switzerland.'

'I've already lost.' His client buried his face in his hands. 'What do I do if I still love her?'

Dante was the last person to offer relationship advice.

'Wrong office,' he said, albeit kindly. He would not kick a man when down.

'Please…' His client looked up. 'Tell me…'

'I've never had a successful relationship nor do I want one.'

'Dante…?'

While he would never offer relationship advice, on occasions such as this, when he was invited to…

'Some mistakes you cannot come back from.'

'It was just once…'

Dante was about to conclude the conversation, but his client was being honest now.

'It was more than once. And I regret my indiscretions more than you could know.'

'Believe me,' Dante corrected with a grim smile. 'I do know.'

'What can I do? Please, just…'

'Okay,' Dante said, and then sat for a moment in silence, considering not an ex-lover, but the loss of his brother. 'Even if hurts, you have to try to let the other go with dignity and grace.'

'What if I can't?'

'Then it ends in court.'

Before his client left his office, Dante offered his hand, as well as one last word of advice. 'Do *not* contact your wife.'

Alone, Dante made his call.

'Hello?' Sev said.

'You asked me to call?'

'Yes, hold on.'

Sev got rid of whoever was with him and switched to video call. Dante stared, unsmiling, into his phone at a slightly older version of himself.

There were differences. Sev's eyes were grey, whereas Dante's were a deep brown, and Dante had a scar through his left eyebrow. And, though their hair was the same thick glossy black, Sev wore his a little longer. Both were tall and broad, and had similar features—strong jaws and straight roman noses. They were clearly cut from the same cloth.

Once Sev had been the more solemn of the two, although now they almost shared that podium…

'How's Dubai?' Dante asked, hating the polite small talk, but attempting to take the dignified route he had suggested to his client.

'Hot,' Sev said, perhaps hating the forced conversation too. 'How are things in Milan?'

'Cold.'

'Just a couple of things to discuss,' Sev said. 'Helene mentioned that you haven't RSVP'd regarding the ball. I can't attend this year.'

'Well, I shan't be going,' Dante responded.

He attended many events representing their grandfather's winery, but the spring ball in Lucca was one he avoided.

'It's important to Gio. We're the main sponsors.'

'We?' Dante provoked. 'I'm not an owner, and neither are you.'

'Dante…' Sev said, in a wry use of his name. Technically their grandfather was the owner, but the brothers dealt with the management of it, and both knew it would eventually pass to them. Hopefully not too soon. 'Have you been able to visit the winery lately?'

Dante stared back at his brother. He loathed going back to Lucca—especially to the winery. He could still see the wreckage in the hills every time he visited.

'No,' he said finally, and, even though they were not talking, he knew it was in moments like this that he wanted conversation. To ask his brother if he shared the same visions, if the nightmare of that day was all he could see whenever he returned home. 'I find it—'

'Inconvenient?' Sev snapped. 'We all know you're busy, Dante. So, when *will* you be back?'

'I don't know,' Dante said, knowing that Sev was now getting to the real reason for this rare call. 'In a couple of weeks, maybe. Why?'

'I called Gio yesterday…unexpectedly.'

Neither brother called him Nonno—and not just because it didn't work well in business matters. Dante, back when he'd had a heart, had been the cheekier of the two and had started to call him by his name. He had been unable to understand why he got told off when he did.

'But he *is* Gio…' he'd said, and hugged his *nonno* so fiercely and called him by his name with such love that it had stuck.

'He seemed a bit vague,' said Sev.

'As do you,' Dante pointed out, for usually their conversations were more specific. 'He struggles with his new phone; though I tried to show him how it worked at Christmas.'

'How was he then?'

'Just Gio being Gio,' Dante said. 'A bit…' He turned his mind back a couple of weeks. 'A bit morose, maybe? He was talking about…' He hesitated, loath to mention the date the brothers hated most. The one time in the year when they were forced together. 'He wanted to start making plans for the ten-year memorial. I told him it was months away. He certainly wasn't vague then.'

Dante's frown deepened as his brother spoke again. 'He was alone. Apparently the domestic staff are off for a couple of extra weeks.'

'Mimi's there, though?' Dante checked, because even if most of the household staff were on leave Mimi, his grandfather's housekeeper, would be there.

'I'm not so sure,' Sev said. 'Dante, he was in his robe and still unshaven at midday.'

'Gio?' Dante shook his head. 'Perhaps he was—'

'I took a screenshot,' Sev said.

'Okay.'

Dante gave the one-word response as he looked at the photo. And Sev, even if they weren't talking, knew his ways. He stayed silent and let Dante think…

His grandfather was a very formal man. Always up with the birds and immaculately dressed for his morning stroll along the walls. This shot of him unshaven and in a robe meant something was wrong.

Still silent, Dante glanced at Sev. For a brief second he felt his brother's eyes on the scar that ran through his eyebrow. The scar Sev had put there. He watched as Sev hastily pulled his eyes back to meet his brother's gaze.

They *never* discussed that time.

'Delete that photo,' Sev warned. 'I'll do the same.'

'I'll go and see him,' Dante told his brother. 'I'll just arrive unannounced.'

'When?'

He knew he had a packed schedule, and a date tonight, yet he had to think hard to remember her name and none of it really mattered, Dante realised.

'Now.'

'It's just a hunch,' said Sev. 'I'm not asking you to drop everything.'

'It's Gio,' Dante responded.

'Yes…'

'Hopefully it's nothing,' Dante said. 'I'll let you know when I've seen him.'

'Thanks.'

There were no goodbyes.

From either of them.

Sev rang off and Dante sat in silence, staring at the image of his grandfather, who seemed to have aged a decade in the past couple of weeks.

He cancelled his date.

Actually, he ended his association with her there and then.

Nothing mattered other than Gio.

He buzzed his PA.

'Change of schedule,' he told Antonia. 'I need to be in Lucca tonight.'

CHAPTER ONE

SUSIE BILTON'S SMILE was present and correct.

Her blonde hair was neatly pinned back. Her black dress was immaculate. And her black apron, with the elegant Pearla's logo spun in gold over one pocket, was neatly tied. She wore the requisite black tights and, because she would be on her feet for the next six hours, black rather sensible shoes.

The team were being briefed by Pedro, the head waiter. But her eyes drifted to the busy kitchen—to Cucou, the head chef, who was laughing as he twirled fresh pasta like a skipping rope.

'Susie?'

'Sorry,' she said, and tore her gaze from the kitchen and back to Pedro.

Having been in Lucca for four weeks, working over Christmas and New Year and taking language courses during the week, Susie understood most of what Pedro said.

'We have a birthday. The cake is a surprise, so don't offer birthday wishes until then. And an engagement.'

He smiled, and so did the staff. The restaurant was on the walls of Lucca, and very elegant, and was often a chosen venue to celebrate precious times.

Pedro took them through the choices on the menu tonight. 'Cucou has prepared a ricotta and spinach ravioli with a walnut sauce...'

Susie found her gaze again drifting to the kitchen, to the slight frenzy taking place as they prepared for a busy night. It was a noisy, busy kitchen, and there were often shouts and sometimes bursts of laughter. She would give anything to be a part of that team...

Maybe one day...

Though not at Pearla's.

When she'd applied to work here, Susie had told the manager that her goal was to work in the kitchen, that she would do anything...

Anything.

Honestly, she'd be happy washing the dishes or peeling onions. Anything to be given a chance in the kitchen of this beautiful five-star restaurant. She didn't understand how they would let her loose on the clients, but not in the kitchen.

Actually, she did understand...

It was the reason she was here.

The really good Italian restaurants, even in England, required you to be fluent in the language to work in the kitchen.

She'd tried learning Italian at home, but her ex had rolled his eyes at her attempts. He hadn't understood how cooking wasn't just work, it was her passion.

She couldn't blame him for that. Not her parents, nor her sisters, and none of her friends understood the frustration she'd felt working as a cook in an Italian restaurant that was part of a large chain. Yes, she'd got to cook—but to a set menu. And it had involved a lot of heating up pre-prepared food, or adding the chain's salad dressing to a standard version of salad. She'd wanted to create her own. But first of all she knew she had to learn...

That was why she was in Lucca, taking lessons each weekday morning at the language school, and to pay her way she was waitressing whenever she got a shift.

'There's also a reduced bar menu,' Pedro was saying, and

Susie felt tension in her jaw as the waiting staff were told the kitchen was short-staffed tonight.

Again.

It was common even at the most exclusive venues.

As the staff dispersed the first customers were starting to enter, but Susie held back.

'Susie…?' Pedro frowned.

'I could help,' she responded in Italian, but she saw the flicker of impatience on Pedro's face. He really didn't have time to listen to her stumble through her words, but surely her Italian had improved since she'd arrived?

'You do help,' he responded in English. 'I know it is irregular, asking you to deliver meals…' He gave a small shudder—food delivery was not usually an option, yet for certain guests exceptions were made! 'Gio—I mean, Signor Casadio—hasn't called yet, but if he does…'

'I meant in the…' Susie started, but then realised that Pedro had perhaps deliberately misunderstood. He knew she wanted a chance in the kitchen—she'd asked often enough!

'Susie…' Pedro sighed. 'Please, there are guests waiting.'

'Of course.'

Burning with a blush, she turned and approached her first table for the night. The guests were English, so no practising her language skills there.

It was a busy Friday night—so busy that her blonde hair started spilling out of its pins, and Pedro sent her to the cloakroom to fix it. In the mirror she saw her flushed face and, very rarely for Susie, the glitter of tears in her vivid blue eyes.

'Susie…?' Her name was being called as she came out. 'Kitchen!'

She felt a lurch of hope—but no, Cucou was putting the finishing touches to the birthday cake. It looked stunning, and had been made by the maestro himself.

She watched as Cucou wiped the edge of the plate.

'Perfect,' he said, more to himself than to Susie.

'It looks far too good to eat.'

Susie smiled, trying to make conversation, to be noticed by Cucou, but he wasn't really listening.

'It's my sisters' birthday today,' she said in Italian, as Pedro lit the candles on the cake. 'I'm sure their cake isn't—'

'Sister!' Pedro abruptly corrected Susie's Italian. '*Her* cake...'

The correction was unnecessary—for once Susie hadn't mixed up her plurals or tenses or whatever. 'No, I meant *sisters*,' she said. 'They're twins.'

For the first time Cucou seemed interested in what Susie had to say. He actually asked her a question. 'Are they identical twins?'

It was the same question everyone asked. *Everyone!*

'*Si,*' Susie said.

And then she stood there, her lips a little pursed, as Pedro and Cucou proceeded to chat about some identical twin brothers who lived nearby. How, even if they came to Pearla's separately, they ordered the same meal, inadvertently dressed the same at times.

Typical, Susie thought as Cucou proudly lifted the cake, that the one time he'd spoken to her it was about her sisters.

Out they all walked, Cucou carrying the cake, and Pedro, Susie and the wine waiter behind with champagne, descending on the couple as the lucky birthday lady let out a cry of surprise and delight.

'How beautiful!' She smiled at her partner. 'You never forget.'

Gosh, she really was teary tonight, Susie realised. Only it wasn't the little party here that was causing her slight upset tonight. It was the little party undoubtedly taking place tonight back in London that had her feeling a little...

It was a feeling she would rather not acknowledge.

Anyway, there wasn't time—the delightful Signor Casadio had again made good use of his new phone and she was to take over his meal.

It had been New Year's Eve when he'd first rung the restaurant.

They had been so busy that all calls were going to the machine, and yet Pedro had been startled when he'd heard his voice and had immediately taken the call.

'Of course, Signor Casadio, it would be our pleasure to bring your meal over.'

Susie had frowned as Pedro had hung up the phone.

'I thought the restaurant didn't deliver?'

'We do when it's Gio Casadio asking,' Pedro had snapped, and then dashed off to speak with Cucou.

Susie had assumed the reason she'd been chosen to deliver to him was because she was new and could most easily be spared. Or possibly they'd been forced to acknowledge that she did have some culinary skills. Susie had been told she must cook the fresh pasta once she was there, serve the meal, grate the truffle and cheese, and suggest a wine from his collection.

'I'll be there for ages,' she'd protested.

'As long as is needed,' Pedro had insisted, seemingly prepared to take the shortfall in staff despite it being New Year's Eve.

And today it was still the case, because now, two weeks on, at around 8:00 p.m., Susie pulled on her trench coat and hastily wrapped a pretty scarf around her neck as Pedro came over with the bags.

'There's also a fruit compote and a light yoghurt.' Pedro dropped his voice. 'For his breakfast tomorrow...'

Susie's smile was more natural now as she nodded—she was loving how they were very discreetly taking care of this elderly man who had found himself home alone.

For reasons the staff would never discuss...

'Do you want to take your break straight after?' Pedro checked.

'Yes,' Susie said. 'Thank you.'

Susie wasn't just delivering a meal. No, she would be preparing coffee for the morning, putting blankets on the couches...just a couple of little jobs in an attempt to help the delightful Signor Gio Casadio.

Stepping out into the cool night, she walked along the gorgeous walls that surrounded the medieval town.

All her life she'd been walking on walls, Susie thought, though none as glamorous as these, treelined and wide. There were dogs being walked, cyclists... She walked on the correct side and looked out to the very old town, saw the Friday night lights and heard the music.

She felt as if she'd been born outside an exclusion zone.

Always on the edge of the real action and gazing longingly in.

Born thirteen months after stunning identical twins, Susie was very used to not turning heads and going unnoticed. Only it wasn't the old ladies beaming at the twins and not at her that had hurt...

Well, it had hurt a bit...

It wasn't even that she'd always felt like an extra at their joint birthday parties...though it had made her feel a bit invisible at times.

As she'd told Cucou, it was their birthday today, and she felt far away from the little party taking place at home. Far from any friends as she stood at the bottom of the career ladder, in a town where she didn't belong, and acknowledged the ache inside her.

Lonely.

She'd always felt it.

'Stop it!' Susie told herself and picked up her pace, refusing to feel sorry for herself.

She had a lot to be happy about. Once her Italian had improved, she would be off to Florence to do a cooking course. And before that her parents were coming to Lucca to spend some time here. Best of all, their visit would coincide with her own birthday.

As for men… With one relationship to her name—one that hadn't worked out—she was alone by choice.

Single and loving it—wasn't that how she was supposed to be feeling?

She came to the huge iron gates of Signor Casadio's vast property—far too big for an elderly man to manage alone.

At the urging of his housekeeper, Susie had arranged for some of the furniture to be moved, fashioning a kind of bedsit arrangement in the dining room, and she adored their chats as she prepared his meals in the attached butler's kitchen and served his dinner—even if he was rather maudlin.

Last night he'd wept with shame because his grandson had called and seen him in his robe…

'I hate this phone,' he'd sobbed. 'I hate it that Sev saw me like that.'

'It's okay,' Susie had said. 'I'm sure he didn't even notice…'

Now she walked up the path, past the fountains and stone benches and bare winter trees, looking up at the dark building and hoping that Gio had heeded her gentle prompts to shave and get dressed.

Walking beneath the portico, she headed around the vast building to the beautiful French windows that led off the dining room. She knocked on the glass and then pushed down the handle, her smile widening in delight when she saw that Gio was indeed dressed and shaved. Not only that, but spread out on the table were necklaces, earrings…the family jewels—and she rather hoped she knew why.

Perhaps Mimi would be getting a ring after all!

Mimi, his housekeeper, had walked out on New Year's Eve, Gio had told her. She wanted more.

At first, Susie had assumed she wanted more money—but no. She'd gleaned from Gio the fact Mimi wanted more acknowledgement...more respect.

And during her daily talks with Mimi, who was keeping an eye on Gio from a distance, via Susie, she'd found out that Mimi wanted to be more than Gio's secret mistress.

Susie had blushed at that.

Gio had told her a little about it too...

'Signor Casadio...' she said now, and smiled.

'Ah, Susie...'

He half stood, and she waved him to sit back down. And then, before Gio had time to inform her, she knew there was another person in the room.

'I have a guest,' Gio said, with a wry edge to his tone. 'Usually, I am informed prior to his arrival.'

'I wasn't aware I needed an invitation.'

The unexpected guest stepped forward.

He was still in his coat, his black hair a little damp from the rain, and had clearly just arrived. It had to be one of the grandsons—Gio had shown her photos of them, though they were all from a long time ago. Before Gio's family had been torn apart by a dreadful tragedy.

She knew she should be relieved that one of the grandsons was finally here.

And in a moment perhaps she would be both pleased and relieved that someone was here for Gio.

First, though, she must attune herself to his beauty.

Her skin had to cool from the blush that had emerged, her mouth had to work out how to move, and she somehow had to step down from the high alert her senses had been placed on.

No photo could truly have prepared her, for it wasn't just his physical beauty, but the dark eyes and the way, though he stood by a wall, he somehow commandeered the room.

'My grandson,' Gio informed her. 'Dante.'

'Oh,' Susie croaked, and then made the foolish mistake of attempting small talk while blindsided by beauty. 'The cheeky one!'

Her little quip dropped like a stone between them.

He wiped the smile from her face with a sharp frown.

It was then that she realised the foolishness of her words. Of talking to this imposing man in the terms Gio had used as he'd reminisced.

Dante was the younger one.

The cheeky one.

The funny one.

The loving one.

She wanted to die. Of all the ridiculous things to say! The impish, cheeky little boy that Gio had spoken about was no-where to be seen. This man's lips were almost scathing, with no trace of a smile, and his eyes were suspicious—as if she were some kind of intruder.

Susie rather wished the marble floor beneath her feet would open up and swallow her.

'Sorry.' She gave her head a shake, wishing she could re-tract what she'd said. She was about to flee to the kitchen, but Gio was speaking again.

'No doubt he is here in Lucca to check up on me.'

'I live here,' Dante said, removing his suspicious gaze from Susie as he addressed his grandfather.

'No,' Gio said, rummaging through the jewels in front of him. 'You live in Milan; you have a property here that stands mostly empty. You forgot about home a long time ago.'

'That's not true, Gio,' Dante said.

There was a slight husk to his voice, and he closed his eyes. Both weariness and pain flickered across his features, and then he spoke on.

'I was here at Christmas, and I'm here now.' His eyes opened then, and he stared at his grandfather. 'Where's Mimi?'

Gio gave no answer.

'I'll sort out dinner,' Susie said into the tense air, and was more than happy to go into the small butler's kitchen. Trying to pretend he didn't affect her so, she attempted to be polite. 'Are you staying to eat?'

'No,' Gio answered for him. 'I'm sure Dante has a date to keep.'

'Yes,' Dante said, his eyes still on his grandfather. 'I shall be staying for dinner.'

'Sure.'

Susie worked quickly, putting on water for the pasta before she'd even removed her scarf, then preparing Gio's Moka pot for the morning, filling it with water and coffee and putting it on the little burner.

She was just unbuttoning her coat when Dante came into the kitchen.

'What's going on?' he asked.

'Sorry?' She gave a nervous half-laugh.

'Why is he here alone?' he demanded in a harsh whisper.

She could hear the accusing tone...as if it were her fault.

'Why didn't you call me?'

'Call you?'

Under his vivid scrutiny she was perplexed by his question, and trying not to notice that his eyes were as brown as chocolate. A very dark chocolate... Certainly they weren't sweet.

'How?'

'You pick up the phone.' He snapped his gaze away and commenced walking around the small kitchen, opening cupboards. 'He's clearly sleeping downstairs; he shouldn't be here alone.'

'I agree, but—'

He wasn't waiting for explanations. Instead he peered into the rather empty fridge. 'There's barely any food in the place.'

And suddenly Susie, who rarely spoke up for herself, decided an exception might well be called for. 'He's *your* grand-father, not mine.' Her voice came out a little more harshly than she'd intended. 'I'm doing what I can.'

She took off her coat, hung it on a hook and felt his eyes drift over her attire and down to her black apron.

'Who *are* you?'

'I work at Pearla's. I'm here delivering an order,' Susie told him.

He didn't respond—just stalked off.

Her heart was thumping as she put the pasta into the water and sliced fresh olive bread, still warm from the oven. Her lips were tense, her shoulders too, as she listened to Dante questioning Gio.

'Where's Mimi?'

'At her sister's.'

'Why?' Dante demanded. 'When did this happen?'

Susie screwed her eyes closed, trying to stay out of it as Gio made some excuse about Mimi wanting a pay rise.

Dante clearly wasn't buying it. 'Then give her more.'

'Don't tell me what to do.'

'Are you living down here?' Dante asked. 'Sleeping in the dining room?'

'It's better to keep only the one room warm,' Gio retorted. 'We have to think of the planet, Dante.'

'Gio! I'm asking seriously, now. What the hell is going on? Sev told me that you were—'

And Susie could stay back no more.

'Ouch!' she yelped, and grabbed a tea towel and wrapped it around her hand. 'Ow...ow...'

Dante came to the door. His coat had been removed and he wore a charcoal-grey suit. His tie was slightly loose, but apart from that he looked dressed for both a stylish office and a photo shoot. Still, as gorgeous as he looked, he was far from sympathetic, and he looked impatiently at her wrapped hand, and then over his shoulder, as if to call for someone.

Clearly he was very used to summoning staff, and she watched as it dawned on him there was no one to summon.

'What's wrong?' Gio called out.

'Nothing, Gio,' she responded. 'Just a little cut.'

'Susie…?' At least Gio was concerned.

'It's fine, Gio,' she called to him. 'Dante's taking care of it.'

Then she met his eyes and mouthed, *Don't!*

'What?'

'Don't mention him being in his robe yesterday,' she whispered.

He frowned, clearly about to turn away and leave her to bleed to death, but then with a slight hiss of frustration he put the conversation with his grandfather on hold and started opening the cupboards, eventually producing a little first-aid box.

'He's embarrassed,' she said in a low tone as he rummaged in the box for a sticking plaster, though he was clearly listening. 'He was devastated that Sev saw him in his dressing gown. I promised Gio that Sev wouldn't have noticed.'

'Okay.' He closed his eyes and inhaled deeply. 'He's dressed and shaved now though?'

'Yes.' She nodded, not wanting to break a confidence and choosing not to tell Dante that she'd gently suggested to Gio that he tidy himself up a bit. 'Just don't tell him Sev noticed.'

'Very well.' He nodded curtly. 'Let's sort out your hand.'

He took her wrapped hand and she noticed the contrast of his olive-skinned fingers against her pale forearm. His hands were cold, his fingers long, and an expensive navy watch face peeked from beneath his cuffs. She watched the sweep of the seconds ticking away, far more slowly than the beat of her heart. His touch was deft and firm, and the effect was both unexpected and unknown…

She watched tiny goosebumps appearing on her own flesh, and her nose seemed to twitch as it was treated to a gorgeous citrussy, spicy scent, as if it were trying to decipher whether it was his skin or his hair that smelt so divine.

Mute at his touch, she stood stock-still as he unwrapped the tea towel and exposed her hand.

'Where?' he asked, turning her hand in his own. 'Where's the cut?' He peered at her blemish-free hand and the clean white tea towel, then let out a mirthless laugh as he realised her ruse. 'Were you faking it?'

'Yes,' Susie said, only her voice sounded strange...as if her throat was inflamed. Actually, it felt a little as if it was. 'Go gently on him.'

He frowned and then, still holding her hand, he lifted his head and met her eyes. She knew from both Gio and Mimi a little of this fractured family's history, and that Dante's arrogance tonight was because he was scared for his grandfather. Gio had been right when he'd said that that Sev would turn up, or Dante. She hadn't really believed him—had privately thought that one dressing gown day wouldn't have his grandsons come running—yet here Dante was.

'He's a bit fragile,' Susie said.

'Yes.' He gave a nod. 'I'll go gently.'

'Good.'

'I'd better put a plaster on you, or he'll notice.'

'Indeed,' she agreed, because Gio was as sharp as a tack.

And so she stood, her heart thumping loudly, as those longfingered hands peeled the backing off a little plaster.

He looked at her pale hands, as if considering where to place it. Then he chose her palm and positioned it over her life line. And as he lightly pressed it into her flesh he unknowingly answered a question that had perplexed her for months...

Why had she ended a seemingly fine two-year relationship? Something had been missing.

She simply hadn't known what.

It had been okay...

But never had she felt this level of attraction.

Pure, unadulterated, physical attraction.

Attraction so immediate and intense that were he to kiss her now it would seem almost appropriate.

She looked to his mouth, and then down to her hand, still held by his, and somehow, rather than kiss his face off, she reclaimed it.

'Thank you,' she said.

'No problem.'

He, of course, seemed entirely unaware of the seismic shift taking place inside her.

'The sauce!' she yelped, certain it must have burnt dry. And yet as she dashed over she saw it was barely close to a simmer. 'I'll put the pasta on and then...' She was trying to recall Cucou's orders. 'Wine...' she said. 'A Sauvignon will pair nicely with...'

'Thank you,' he said, with a slightly wry edge.

He left the kitchen then.

Thank goodness!

Soon she was bringing out plates. They were both seated at the very large dining table and that pleased her, because before Gio had been eating on the sofa. He looked brighter for the company, Susie thought.

Dante must have been to the main kitchen, and was now pouring wine.

'Thank you,' he said as she put down the plates. As she went to offer cheese, he took the grater. 'I've got it,' he said, and grated cheese over Gio's dinner.

She tidied up the kitchen and filled the sink with hot soapy water, as she did every time, then fetched her coat, pleased to hear the low hum of conversation and even the sound of Gio's laughter as she pulled it on.

'I'd better get back…' she told them. 'The restaurant's really busy.'

'Is your hand okay?' Gio checked.

'It's fine.' She held up her palm and showed him the plaster. 'Just a tiny cut.'

She wrapped her scarf around her neck and stepped out into the night, grateful for the chilly air, certain her face was on fire.

It was a relief to close the large gates behind her and step onto the walls.

She'd have liked to sit for a moment, just to relive that moment when time had seemed to slow down…when everything had stopped. To sit for a moment and dwell on a pompous, arrogant man who clearly loved his grandfather deeply.

Oh, she hoped he'd tread gently.

Thanks to Susie's acting skills Dante was treading gently.

'You said you spoke to Sev…?' said Gio warily, resuming the conversation once Susie had left.

Dante was grateful that she'd interrupted him. The last thing he wanted to do was embarrass his grandfather.

'What did Sev say?'

'That he can't make the ball.'

'Can you?'

'No.' Dante shook his head.

'But a Casadio has to be there.'

'Could you go?' Dante asked, wondering if this might be his way into a rather awkward conversation.

'No, that was where I proposed to your *nonna*…'

'I know,' Dante said. 'But…'

He wanted to point out that that had been a very long time ago, but he knew it wouldn't go down well, so he gave up on that suggestion.

'I really can't,' he said. 'I've got a big case that looks as if it's heading for court.'

'You mean a divorce?' His grandfather's lips curled slightly. 'Marriage is sacred.'

'If I was a criminal defence lawyer, would you blame me for my clients' sins?'

'I guess not.' Gio gave a reluctant laugh. 'Who's the client?'

'I'd rather not discuss it.'

Dante did not bring his work life to the dinner table, and although Gio would only have to glance at the news in a few weeks' time to find out who his grandson was representing, Dante would not be the one to tell him.

Gio had more immediate concerns. 'What else did Sev say?'

'Not much.'

'It's good to know you two occasionally talk.'

'Of course we speak.'

'Dante!' Gio rebuked. 'I might be old, but I am no fool. You two haven't spoken since…'

He paused, but they'd had this discussion many times over the years, so Dante was certain Gio had been about to refer to the accident.

'Grief affects people differently,' Dante said. 'Sev lost his wife and—'

'And you two fell out long before the accident.'

There was a clatter as Gio threw down his cutlery and broke the unspoken rule of the Casadio men left behind, venturing into territories that by mutual silent consent they all avoided.

'The night before Sev and Rosa married the two of you fought…' He got up and took down a photo, holding it out in front of Dante. 'You didn't get that scar from falling while celebrating! And Sev's hand was so swollen from hitting you, Rosa couldn't get his wedding band on. I didn't believe you then and I don't believe you now. You said something to Sev about Rosa, didn't you?'

Dante almost lost his poker face, inwardly startled by his grandfather's question, but he had trained himself well and kept his features impassive as he responded. 'I just asked him if he was certain that marriage was what he wanted.'

'Why?' Gio demanded.

Dante twisted the last of his pasta on his fork, even as the knife in his heart twisted tighter. Gio had loved Rosa, he was certain. There was no way he could tell him that two years prior to the wedding he'd slept with Rosa—nor that she'd told him she might be pregnant in an attempt to trap him and that night he'd been concerned Rosa might be playing the same tricks on Sev.

Instead, he offered a very diluted version of his thoughts around that time. 'I thought I was looking out for him.'

Gio made a small hissing noise that said what he thought of Dante's actions. 'You should never come between a man and his choice of bride.'

'I know that now!' Dante said tartly. 'Thanks for the late advice.'

To his surprise there was a small burst of laughter from Gio, but then his face flicked back to serious. 'You should have come to me.'

Dante responded with a thin smile.

'Did Sev tell you I was looking unkempt?' asked Gio.

'What?' Dante feigned a frown.

'Dante...?'

Had it not been for Susie he would have answered honestly—after all, Gio had invited him to speak. But he looked at his proud grandfather and heeded her plea to tread gently.

'I have no idea what you are talking about. What do you mean "unkempt"?'

'I didn't know it was a video call. Sev caught me at the wrong time.'

'Okay.' Dante thought for a moment before he responded. 'You're looking very smart now. Are you feeling better?'

'Somewhat.' He nodded. 'Susie said if I shaved and put on my best clothes I might feel like going for a walk...'

'Did you?'

'No, but I did take out the jewellery...'

'So I see.'

He glanced to the coffee table, at the necklaces, bracelets and rings all strewn across it.

'What else have you been doing?'

'Not much.'

'Can you tell me what's wrong?'

'Like you, there are things I would prefer not to discuss.' Gio moved the topic on. 'How long are you home for?'

'I'm here all weekend. So I can do whatever needs doing.'

'The dishes tonight?'

'I can give it a go.' Dante's smile was wry. 'I'll sort out a temporary housekeeper tomorrow.'

'I don't need that.' He looked at Dante. 'If you want to help, then pay a visit to the winery. I haven't been able to get there...' He frowned. 'I know you don't want anything to do with the place, and I'm sure you and your brother will sell it the second I'm gone, but while I am alive—'

'Gio,' Dante cut in. 'I care about the place.'

'How?' Gio asked. 'How can you care for it from Milan?'

'Okay, I'll go,' Dante agreed, even though it was the last place he wanted to visit.

The helicopter had taken off from there, and it was there where everyone had gathered, waiting for news, or confirmation, watching the fire in the hills. Even the drive there was hell now, winding past churches where weddings and funerals had taken place.

'What else can I do?' he asked.

'I have to sort out the jewels. They haven't been cleaned and I—'

'I'll take them to someone in Milan,' Dante cut in.

But Gio instantly declined. 'No! I want them to be taken care of here, where I had them made.'

'Fine.' Dante nodded. 'Gio, can I ask if Mimi is coming back?'

'I don't know,' Gio said.

Dante watched as his grandfather fought with himself, perhaps wanting to talk, yet refusing to.

'You said you would do the dishes,' he said eventually.

'Sure.'

Dante collected the two plates and took them through to the butler's kitchen. Not completely useless, he went to put them in the dishwasher—but then he saw the sink filled with soapy water.

She'd filled the sink for Gio, he realised.

That was kind of her.

She *was* kind, he realised.

For the first time in ages...perhaps since university...he did the dishes, rinsed the glasses, then walked back to the dining room that had somehow turned into his grandfather's bedsit.

'Are you going?' Gio asked.

'I think so.'

'I was going to watch a film...'

God help me, Dante thought as he sat on the sofa with a large brandy watching Sophia Loren, ever beautiful, in black and white.

'Your *nonna* loved this.'

'I know.'

Because Gio had repeatedly told him.

His gaze drifted from the screen and he noticed the changes since Christmas: more photos had been moved here, as well as the television and his grandfather's old gramophone. Most confusing, though, they were seated on the heavy couches that belonged in the formal lounge, and there were blankets folded on one.

'How did the couches get in here?' Dante asked.

'Susie,' Gio said.

'How?' Dante asked. 'She's tiny.'

But Gio didn't answer. He was gazing at the voluptuous Sophia, obviously thinking of Nonna.

Dante's mind drifted to the rather slender waitress who had somehow rescued the night.

'You should have spoken to me first,' Gio said suddenly, pulling him from his thoughts.

Dante looked at the screen and saw the film was over. 'When?' He frowned.

'If you were worried about Rosa, you should have come to me rather than go to your brother.'

'Leave it, Gio…' Dante warned.

Oh, it really was time to go.

He stood and retrieved his coat. 'I'll come over tomorrow, before going to the winery.'

'Dante, please…you should have come to me.'

'Gio…' His eyes briefly closed in weariness, but before he could go on Gio spoke again.

'I had my reservations about the marriage, too.'

Dante was sure he'd misheard, and was almost scared to move in case he reacted too much only to find out he'd got things wrong. He was a master of the impassive, yet it took him a full second to wipe the flash of shock from his features before meeting Gio's eyes.

'But you loved Rosa!'

'I love Sev,' Gio said. 'And because of that I tried to care for Rosa. But I was sure her family were trying to get their hands on my winery.'

'Did you ever share those reservations with Sev?'

'Never.' Gio shook his head. 'Only now—only with you.'

'Good,' Dante said. 'Because as it turned out he loved her.' He pointed to his scar. 'It's better that you didn't say anything. When I questioned the marriage, it broke us.'

'You told him you thought her family had pushed for the marriage?'

'I suggested it as a possibility,' Dante agreed.

'What made you suspicious?'

That he would not be revealing to Gio. His grandfather had been a one-woman man, and had long disapproved of Dante's rather casual ways. He didn't need to know that he'd once slept with Rosa...nor the rest of the sordid tale.

And Sev must never know.

'Just a hunch,' Dante settled for saying. 'I was studying property mergers...succession laws.' He shrugged. 'Goodnight.' He kissed his grandfather's cheeks. 'I'll see you tomorrow. Let's hope for a better day.'

He walked along the walls, his collar up against the cold, and called Sev.

'He's okay,' Dante said to Sev's message bank. 'But Mimi seems to have left. Gio won't discuss it, of course, but there's a girl who's been helping...'

He paused, thinking how terse he'd been with Susie. How tonight could have gone so differently had she not faked a small injury. And on this dark night his face moved into a slight smile.

'I'm staying for the weekend; I'll hopefully know more tomorrow.'

Actually, he hoped to know more tonight.

Dante walked further along the treelined walls, loathing being back more with every step, for there were memories everywhere...

'Dante!'

He could almost hear Rosa calling to him, the sound of her

heels as she ran to catch him, and he recalled his annoyance that two years on from their one-night stand she still tried to leap on him when he was home from university.

'Dante, please.'

He walked faster, but it was as if the past was chasing him tonight.

'We need to talk.'

Rosa had grabbed at his arm, but he'd shaken her off.

'There's nothing to talk about,' he'd told her. *'Seriously, Rosa. Stay the hell away.'*

'Dante, you have to listen to me...' she'd urged. *'There's to be an announcement tonight. Sevandro and I are getting engaged.'*

On a hot summer's day he'd felt the blood in his veins turn to ice. The music festival had been on, and he'd been able to hear the music from the valley beneath pounding, to see the revellers everywhere, and somehow he had known in that moment that his life would never be the same...

'No.' He'd shaken his head. *'Sev's never so much as mentioned you.'* She didn't even call him by the name family and friends used. *'No.'*

'It's sudden.' Rosa had nodded. *'Sevandro spoke to my father yesterday. Dante, please, he cannot know about us.'*

'There never was an "us",' Dante had reminded her—as he had many times before.

Usually she begged him to reconsider, but on that day she'd agreed.

'It was a one-off.' She'd taken a deep breath, blinking back fake tears. *'Sevandro can never know. You mustn't tell him.'*

'You don't get to dictate our conversations.'

Then he'd looked at the woman whom he knew had tried to get him to commit by using the oldest trick in the book.

'Are you telling Sev that you're pregnant?'

'Don't be so personal!'

'Personal?' Dante had checked. *'This* is *personal—Sev's my brother.'*

'And your brother is in love with me,' Rosa had said, her voice defiant rather than pleading, no sign of tears. *'Sevandro loves me. If you tell him what once took place, such a long time ago...'* She'd shrugged. *'Take it from me, Dante, you will lose your brother.'*

Perhaps he should have listened to Rosa, Dante thought now as he came to Pearla's and leant on the archway nearby.

While he hadn't told Sev what had taken place between himself and Rosa, he'd tried to broach the topic. He'd used the same excuse he'd given his grandfather tonight, only with a slight twist. He'd told Sev he was studying family law.

To no avail.

On the eve of the wedding he'd been a little more direct, implying that Rosa was trying to force his hand, and that if Rosa was telling him she was pregnant...

He hadn't even finished speaking before Sev had knocked him out cold. Dante would wear the scar of that attempt at conversation for ever.

And Rosa had been right.

He'd lost his brother...

'Ciao, Susie...'

The sound of the name hauled him from dark memories. Glancing over, he saw Susie walking out of Pearla's. Her coat was open. She tied her scarf, then stood opening and closing her umbrella, which seemed to want to invert...

'Susie?'

She put her umbrella up before looking at him. 'We meet again.'

'And not by chance,' he said. 'I would like to apologise...'

CHAPTER TWO

'*SUUU-ZEEE...*'

Somehow Dante made her name sound sexy.

She'd known it was him before she'd even looked over, and her broken umbrella had felt easier to control than the flurry of butterflies escaping in her chest.

She gave him her best version of brisk as her umbrella snapped up into an imperfect shape. 'We meet again,' she said.

'And not by chance.'

Oh, he was actually here to see her!

'I would like to apologise.'

'Apologise?' Susie checked, so stunned to see him waiting for her that she forgot to be shy. 'You mean for being rude earlier?'

'Yes,' he agreed, and she thought he almost smiled.

She'd heard of people taking your breath away, but he took more than that, and for a second she wasn't capable of words, or even of walking off. She was choosing to prolong the encounter, only she did not know what to say.

He solved that with a question. 'How's the "cut" on your hand?'

'Much better.' She held up her unblemished palm, the plaster gone. 'I heal quickly.'

'You do.' He nodded.

It was the oddest moment of her life. He was looking at her, and the conversation was pleasant, yet she actually recalled that moment where he'd touched her hand, and how his touch had made her heart seem to flutter in her throat.

It felt the same now.

He couldn't have noticed, of course, for she just stood there, a little stunned at her own thoughts, as Dante spoke on.

'I overreacted. Sev had called me and I was expecting...' He gave a helpless shrug. 'I don't even know what I was expecting.'

'I get it.' She nodded. 'It's nice that you came to check on him.'

'Always,' he said. 'I'll stay for the weekend and try and sort a few things out for him. It's kind of you to have helped. Also, we need to discuss money.'

'We don't.' Susie flushed.

'You're English,' he said. 'So I know discussing money is painful for you.'

She laughed, just a little bit, but it was enough that she relaxed a little and could look him in the eye. 'Seriously, there's no need.'

Her lips pressed closed. She did not want to reveal the arrangement she had with Mimi.

'You're clearly doing more than just dropping off meals.'

'I'm not.'

'So you get the morning coffee ready for all your clients. Fill the sink? Move furniture?'

'No,' she admitted. 'But I really don't do much.' She gave a small shake of her head. 'I don't think Gio would appreciate this conversation.'

'Perhaps not, but *I* would appreciate knowing what is going on.' He relented a little. 'I want to help him, too.'

'I know...' She hesitated, not wanting to break her new friend's confidence. 'Look, I just do a little here and there...

not much at all. I think…' She looked at his pale face, his dark eyes, and for a second all thought stopped.

'You think…?' he persisted.

'That I should go,' Susie said. 'It's late…'

Somehow he made her want to be indiscreet. And not just with Gio's secrets. He took the cold air away; he made the night somehow shiny.

'It was a long shift,' she added.

'Of course.' He nodded. 'Where do you live?'

She pointed in the direction of her apartment.

'I'll say goodnight, then. Again, I am sorry for earlier.'

He gave her a nod and walked off, and Susie stood there, a little unsure what to do. Her apartment might be where she'd pointed, but her favourite ice-cream shop was in the direction Dante was headed!

And after a very long shift she wasn't missing her treat.

She gave him a small head start and then followed him along the pathway, hoping he wouldn't notice…

Dante didn't notice her at first.

It wasn't her clumpy shoes that had him turning around. More that he turned to catch another glimpse of the woman, Susie, who been the sole reason he'd smiled a few times today.

And then he saw her—a few steps behind him.

He frowned, and got back to walking, but he could hear her footsteps now, so he turned again.

'I'm not following you,' she told him. 'I like to get an ice cream at the end of my shift.' She'd caught up with him now. 'I think about it all night.'

'Do you?'

'Yes.'

'What flavour?'

'I don't know yet,' Susie told him as they took the steps

down from the walls. 'I'm trying to work my way through the list, but I adore the red velvet.'

'Then get the red velvet, surely?'

'I want to try new things. My ice-cream-at-night habit only began when I started working at Pearla's.'

'When was that?'

'I've been there a month now. I started a week after I arrived.'

She told him she was here studying the language.

'And I'm off to Florence soon, to do a cookery course, but I have to be fluent to do that... I'm going for total immersion.' She looked over to him then. 'I ought to be speaking to you in Italian.'

'*Lieto di accontentarla,*' he said, but then he saw her slight frown and translated. 'Happy to oblige.'

'Thank you, but please, no...' She drooped. 'It's nearly midnight and my brain's a bit fried.' She peered over at him. 'I'm sorry, too.'

'For what?'

'I was mean.'

'When?'

'When I said about Gio being *your* grandfather...'

'He *is* my grandfather—and you were right to stick up for yourself. That's not being mean.'

'It felt mean.'

'Not in my world,' he said, but she wasn't listening.

He saw her eyes actually light up—clearly the ice cream had come into view. Her chosen venue was popular, because even this late there were people lining up in the street.

'Do you want one?' she offered.

Dante was about to decline, and tell her he wasn't a fan of ice cream, but he'd already been rude enough.

'Let me get these.'

'No, no...'

'It's an ice cream, Susie,' he pointed out. 'What flavour?'

'Oh, God!' She looked at the board, as anxious as if he'd demanded the answer to some impossible mathematical equation. 'Pistachio,' she said. 'Actually, no... Espresso...' She shook her head.

'Red velvet?' he checked, and she gave a resigned nod.

'I'm so predictable,' she sighed as he ordered. 'What are you getting?'

Amareno,' Dante said. 'Sour cherry.'

Soon they stood with their chosen ice creams. He could see her eyes on his.

'Thank you,' she said.

'You're welcome.'

'Well, I'm that way...' She gestured with her head. 'Goodnight.'

'Buona notte.'

Oh, my...

Her brain certainly wasn't too fried to appreciate being wished goodnight in silky Italian by someone so delicious.

Susie walked off with her treat and a whole barrage of new sensations, and wished Gio had warned her how devastatingly handsome his youngest grandson was...

'Susie?'

She was barely two steps into her journey home when he halted her.

'Can I ask one question?'

She turned around and stood a short distance apart from him. He was beautiful in the rain. 'You can ask...although whether or not I'll answer...'

'How did you move the furniture?'

She let out a small laugh and then beneath her umbrella, ice-cream cone in hand, she flexed her arm. 'I'm deceptively strong.'

He nodded, but instead of leaving it was Susie who now prolonged things. 'I also have a question.'

'Go ahead.'

'You said I should have called you. How?'

'You pick up your phone.' He shrugged and stared back at her for what felt like a full moment.

A moment during which her toes curled in her clumpy shoes and she gripped her umbrella as if it were a pole that might secure her against walking towards him.

'But I didn't know who you were...where you worked, or...'

'It would have taken two minutes to find out.'

'Please...' she retorted, disbelieving him. 'Goodnight, Dante.'

This time she walked away, but he'd conjured up so many questions that he'd made her giddy.

Her ice cream was especially delicious, even if it wasn't sour cherry, and it was completely devoured by the time she pushed in the code for the vast door of her apartment block.

She collapsed her umbrella and left it in the stand, then climbed the many steps and opened up her door, catching sight of her reflection in the large hall mirror as she did so.

Her face was flushed and her eyes were glittery and she looked as if she'd been very thoroughly kissed. In fact, she was breathing as if she had been, and she couldn't quite blame the stairs!

Her flatmates were either asleep or out, so Susie took herself to her bedroom and flopped down on her bed.

Bewildered.

More than that, fascinated.

She started scrolling through her phone.

Yes, it took less than two minutes for her to find him, but even so... As if this suave, accomplished attorney would have called some lowly waitress back. As if her message would even have been passed on.

Feeling curious, and oddly liberated, she dialled the number of his law firm.

'Hello…' She spoke into a machine. 'My name's Susie Bilton. I'd like to speak to Dante Casadio.' She swallowed as she said what she might have said had she considered calling him about Gio. 'It's a personal matter.'

She rang off and spent the next few moments looking at images on her phone. Staring at the many, many beauties who had accompanied this man on many, many glamorous nights out.

As if he'd even get her message!

Dante quickly relieved himself of his ice cream at the request of a beggar.

'Please,' Dante said, handing it to him. 'Enjoy.'

He was soon at his residence, at the top of Corso Garibaldi.

Usually he would have alerted his part-time housekeeper that he was coming home. Perhaps that was the reason for the unlived-in air as he stepped into his immaculate home. His case was still in the entrance hall, where he'd dropped it off before heading straight to Gio's. There were no lights on…no drinks or food left out…

Not home.

This had been an empty shell when he'd bought it. Rather like himself. Over the years it had been restored to its original glory, yet it brought him no joy, no peace. If anything, the more beautiful it got, the more it reminded him of how hollow he felt. And now it served just as a reminder of the silent commitment he had made to keep a residence here as long as Gio lived.

After that…

Dante was far from naïve, and he knew Gio was getting on. Of course he worried about him. But there'd always been Mimi…

He knew Mimi was not just the housekeeper, but had gone

along with Gio. He always gave notice before he went over, and never commented on the many little things he noticed.

But now clearly his grandfather was unhappy, and Dante knew he had to address it.

How?

He went to the sink and washed his hands, sticky from the ice cream. His intention to garner more information had proved futile. While he admired Susie's discretion, it irked him that she'd told him nothing.

If he saw her tomorrow then he would speak to her again. Directly this time.

He'd ask what she knew about the situation, and not get waylaid with language schools, cooking courses in Florence or ice-cream flavours...

Dante rarely got waylaid.

Susie had called herself predictable.

Oh, no.

Susie was far from that.

CHAPTER THREE

Susie awoke to the bleep of her phone and ignored it.

Then her flatmate Juliet's violin practice commenced, so she buried her head under the covers. Especially when Juliet's bow, or whatever it was called, kept missing certain notes.

The same notes.

Over and over.

She shared the apartment with Juliet, who was English, and Louanna, who was a local.

It was Saturday, and she was determined to have a lie-in. There were no Italian classes at the weekends and nowhere she needed to be until she met Mimi later this morning.

Should she have told Dante that Mimi was giving her daily private Italian lessons so that she could keep an eye on Gio from a distance?

No, because Gio didn't want his grandsons knowing about his relationship with Mimi.

Dante…

He dropped into her consciousness as she tried to sink back into sleep.

What would he say if he knew that Mimi had walked out on Gio because she was tired of being passed off as his house-keeper?

Surely he already knew?

Those knowing brown eyes wouldn't miss much.

Susie lay on her side, her own eyes determinedly closed, and yet he refused to exit the stage of her mind. If anything, the spotlight shone brighter upon him, highlighting the scar above one of those knowing eyes.

Gio had shown her a photo of Sev and Rosa's wedding, so she knew the injury was from then. And Mimi had told her how fractured the brothers' relationship was now.

She recalled how he'd frowned as he'd pulled back the tea towel on her hand, and his slight smile as he'd realised there was no cut... How her skin had turned into goosebumps and she'd held her breath as he'd attended to her fake wound...

Louanna's rather loud voice cut into her lovely sleepy recall, as she informed anyone who wanted to know that coffee was ready, then thankfully the violin stopped.

Susie had given up on sleep now and reached for her phone, delighted to see she had a message in the little Sisters Group they shared—a short message with a link attached.

So excited!

Frowning, muzzy from sleep, she was about to click on the link—it looked like an estate agent's advert—when the message was deleted.

It took her a moment to realise that she'd been sent the message by mistake.

It happened now and then—and it hurt every time. This message perhaps more than most. She'd already guessed from a couple of things her mum had said that the twins were thinking about sharing a flat.

The rapidly deleted message only confirmed it.

She could hear Juliet and Louanna chatting and laughing in the kitchen, and even though they were lovely Susie felt a bit of an outsider.

It wasn't just the fact that she was a temporary housemate

that kept her a little apart from them. Music was her flatmates' energy and their main topic of conversation.

It reminded her of when she was younger, listening to her sisters chatting in the next room.

Gosh, she'd felt left out.

Every night it had sounded as if there was a little party going on, with her listening as Celia and Cassie chatted and giggled or, in later years, cried about a broken heart or whatever...

She was going to go out for breakfast, Susie decided, and speak Italian all day.

No exceptions!

She pulled on some thick black tights and a black jumper, and then wriggled into a burnt orange corduroy pinafore that added a blaze of colour, determined to cheer up and stop being so mopey.

'*Buongiorno!*' Susie breezed into the kitchen.

'Good morning,' Louanna smiled. 'How was...?'

'Ah-ah!' Susie halted her with her hand. '*Italiano.*'

Louanna obliged, telling her that her dress was very colourful and she had a passion for orange. Or something along those lines. Then she asked if she was working tonight.

Susie affirmed that she was, and said that, yes, the restaurant had been busy last night.

'Do you know Mimi?' Louanna asked, as if surprised. 'I saw you with her in a café.'

'Yes.' Susie nodded. It wasn't just her lack of vocabulary that had her holding back from mentioning Gio. She didn't think Gio would like having his personal life discussed, so she'd never mentioned the home deliveries. 'She's helping with my Italian.'

Louanna turned to Juliet. 'Mimi was once a very famous opera singer.'

'Wow...' Juliet said. 'I love opera.'

And back to talking about music they went...

* * *

The rain had dried up, though Susie's trench coat and scarf were still required as the weather was crisp. Still, the sky was the palest blue, and the clearest it had been since her arrival, and it was wonderful to wander through the laneways.

Unexpectedly, she had fallen in love with Lucca.

She meandered through the ancient cobbled streets, just drinking in her surroundings.

She went past the gorgeous opera house, where Mimi had once performed... She would love to go to the opera. It was something she'd never considered before, but here in the birthplace of Puccini it was everywhere.

All roads seemed to lead to the Piazza dell'Anfiteatro, a public square in the heart of Lucca, and she entered it through one of the archways. It was more like a circle, surrounded by tall pastel buildings—an amphitheatre where gladiators had fought. Now, where once the audience had watched on, it was cafés and restaurants, umbrellas and tables.

Wandering around the perimeter, she was soaking it all in while trying to select where to stop for breakfast.

'Hey...'

Susie stilled, the deep voice causing her to startle, and she looked over to the stunning sight of Dante, seated at a café table, sipping coffee and looking rather too gorgeous for a lazy Saturday. He wore a black jumper that must be cashmere, and even dressed casually he looked groomed and elegant. And he was beckoning for her to go over.

Susie went.

'We meet again,' she said, and smiled.

'Everyone meets here,' he informed her.

'How was the sour cherry?' Susie asked.

'Like sour cherries,' he replied, and gestured to his table. 'Would you like to join me?'

'So long as you're not going to interrogate me about Gio,'

she said. But even though he made no promises not to do so, she took a seat.

'I was just about to order.' He signalled to the waiter.

'Is there a menu?'

'No need. I was just getting pastries, bread…'

Susie frowned. 'For all you know I might be gluten intolerant.'

'Then you shouldn't have had that cone last night,' Dante said, then conceded, 'I'll ask for a menu.'

'It's fine.'

Gosh, he was confident. Or perhaps it was just the way things were done here, she mused as he ordered for both of them.

The waiter commented on the gorgeous morning and Dante nodded. Then he attempted to draw Dante into conversation and said how nice it was to see him back…

'Thank you.'

He was rather terse with the waiter, which Susie thought was a bit of a red flag, so she pursed her lips as he shut down the conversation, but when the waiter had gone she spoke up.

'He's just making conversation,' she said. 'Believe me, I know how hard that can be.'

'I went to school with him,' Dante said. 'He was nosey even then.'

'Oh!' She gave a half laugh. 'Sorry. I thought you were being rude. I didn't know there was history.'

'There is history on every corner. You wait—we shall soon be the talk of the town.'

'I'd love to be the talk of the town,' Susie said, and sighed. 'It's my ambition.'

He offered a polite smile at her little joke, but then frowned. 'You're not joking, are you?'

'I'm not,' she agreed. 'I'm sure I'd soon tire of it, but…' She smiled at the very gorgeous Dante. 'Just once.'

'It's actually quite easy to achieve here,' he said. Taking a bread roll, he tore it, then dipped it in honey. 'Aren't we supposed to be speaking in Italian?'

'Not on a Saturday,' Susie lied, forgetting her earlier vow. She wanted to concentrate on the conversation, not on the language. She didn't want to be stilted with Dante. 'It's nice to have a day off—at least from classes.'

'Well, I'm glad to have caught you. I did want to thank you.'

'You already have.' She shrugged.

'Susie, I know about Gio and Mimi. At least, I think I do.'

'What about them?' she asked.

Dante admired the fact that she remained discreet.

'I've long since guessed she is more than a housekeeper.'

Still Ms Discreet said nothing.

'Gio doesn't know I know.'

She met his eyes then, and he saw more than blue. He saw the curiosity that danced in them, and he saw the softness of her lips as they asked an unrelated question.

'Sev's the older brother?'

'The serious one,' he said, watching her blush as she perhaps recalled her comment last night. 'What about you?' he asked, those blue eyes steering him off track and forgetting his intention to be more direct.

'Me?' Susie checked.

'Do you have siblings?'

'Two sisters. They're—' She abruptly halted and Dante couldn't fathom why.

'Older or younger?' he probed.

'Older.'

'You're the baby?'

'Hardly.'

'I meant the favourite.'

'I wouldn't go that far...' She rolled her eyes. 'You're an attorney?'

He nodded. 'My speciality is family law. According to Gio, I do the devil's work.'

'Oh!' Her eyes widened in slight surprise. 'You must hear some tales.'

'I try not to.'

'How could you avoid it?'

'We have a large practice. I deal with the division of assets. Passing the tissues is not my forte.'

She laughed at that, and he found that he smiled as they chatted.

And not about Gio.

He saw now the honey tint to her pale blonde hair and noticed the pretty curl of her fair lashes. She wore the coat she'd had on last night and the same scarf. Because they were seated outside, he did not know how she was dressed beneath.

He recalled her slight figure as she'd removed her coat last night. And he remembered, because he'd held her hand when she'd pretended to cut it, the scent of her hair.

Dante found himself in an unexpected guessing game, wondering not just about the clothes beneath the coat, but also about what colours they might be. She'd been in her uniform last night, and today he found himself searching for clues.

It was something he did at work, of course, and in the courtroom at times—trying to fathom the person he was about to question or challenge.

Only this wasn't work.

And Susie was nothing like the women he dated—sophisticated women who knew that his black heart remained closed and that the only place Dante Casadio lasted was in the bedroom.

He caught her gaze and, to his own surprise, when she smiled so did he.

He didn't usually.

Smile.

And if his phone hadn't beeped he might have studied a little more deeply the shades of blue in her eyes.

'Damn...' He glanced at his phone. '*Scusi*, I have to...'

'Of course.'

He left the table to take the call and she sat there, looking out to the square. She felt the waiter looking over, so resisted checking her reflection in her phone.

Gosh, this morning felt thrilling.

She had to meet Mimi soon, and usually she loved their hour together, but this morning she was tempted to cancel... just for more moments with Dante...

'Sorry about that.'

His voice, though it was now familiar, still made her jump.

'It's fine.'

'No, it's not.'

He let out a low, wry laugh and took a sip of coffee, and then he looked up at her eyes, and then down to the full lips that had stayed closed when he'd pushed for information on his grandfather. Somehow he simply knew she was discreet.

'I have a client... My last words to him were, "Don't contact your wife." Hah!'

'I'm assuming he didn't take your advice?'

'He did not.'

He reached for his coffee, to take another sip, yet even as he lifted the small cup he replaced it.

Was it her patient silence that gave him pause, or was it that she didn't demand information?

Or was it something about sitting beneath the umbrellas in

Piazza dell'Anfiteatro on this gorgeous Saturday with her gentle conversation and beauty that had his guard down a touch.

'He got drunk last night and wrote a six-page letter admitting his failings, offering to change.'

'Oh!' She gave a small giggle.

'And he mailed it.' He hissed in annoyance. 'If he'd sent an email I could at least have read it.'

'Do you read a lot of love letters?'

'Only if I'm being paid to,' he said, and now she really laughed.

The bigger surprise for Dante was that he wanted to tell her more.

Without names or identities, of course…

Perhaps that was it, he pondered.

Susie was from England.

After this weekend he would never see her again.

'I told him yesterday to stay back,' he went on. 'I knew it could only cause trouble. People say and do things they regret when they're upset.'

'I don't.'

Her response caused him to frown, his eyes narrowing, and he leant forward a little in an invitation for her to elaborate.

'I just go quiet.'

'In relationships. Or…?' Dante knew he was fishing.

'In everything, really. Work, family…'

Fishing did not suit Dante. He moved to being direct.

'Are you in a relationship?'

'No.' She gave a tight shrug. 'Not any more.'

God, but he wanted her to elaborate. Instead, she asked about him.

'You?'

'I don't do relationships.'

She lifted her eyes to his and he knew now was the time to make his position absolutely clear.

'I don't get involved with my dates.'

'How can you date and not get involved?'

'Because they are all very short-lived.'

'So, you've never been serious with anyone?'

'Never,' he told her. 'Nor will I ever be.'

'Wow... I'm sure you've broken a lot of hearts.'

'Oh, no.' He shook his head. 'A good time is had by all,' he said, in a low, silky voice. 'So long as both parties agree. Dinner...a nice night...'

'Hey,' the waiter said, bringing out another coffee, his smile aimed now at Susie. 'I didn't catch the name of your English friend...'

'Susie.'

Dante's smile was tight. He loathed the implication—but of course there was. Because he'd never sat in this square with a woman. He'd never brought his dates here. Even as a teenager he'd known to keep all that well away from home, where gossip flared and no forbidden deed went unnoticed.

And so he cut the gossip straight off. 'She has been helping out with Gio.'

'Ah...'

Susie felt the relegation from casual coffee date to Gio's housekeeper or nurse.

She'd thought they'd been flirting—just a bit—but it dawned on her then. The real reason Dante had been hoping they'd catch up. He probably wanted to ask her if she'd be Gio's temporary housekeeper.

No, she did not want to be on Dante's payroll.

Her heart sank.

Of course someone as suave and utterly gorgeous as Dante wasn't going to be seeing her in any way other than as an employee.

'Susie, I was wondering—'

'Please don't,' she broke in. 'The answer's no.'

Frowning with curiosity he met her eyes, as if he hadn't expected Susie to address their situation so boldly.

'I'm very happy at the restaurant.'

'Sorry?'

'You were going to offer to pay me to check in on Gio, or...'

'No.' Dante shook his head. 'That wasn't my question.'

'Good.' She let out a small laugh. 'I adore him, but...'

'I get it.' He took a sip of coffee.

'No,' Susie said—because it wasn't that she didn't want to help Gio, and frankly she needed any work she could get. 'I think of Gio as a friend. I like our chats and helping out. I don't want to get paid for it.'

'Susie, that wasn't my question.'

'What was it, then?' she asked, certain it would be something about Gio.

'Would you like to go for dinner tonight?'

'Dinner?' Susie frowned. 'To talk about your grandfather?'

'Oh, no.'

She swallowed. The café's heaters must have suddenly been turned up, because she was boiling beneath them. Truly. She wanted to fling off her coat or tip a bucket of ice over her head.

Never had she been so boldly propositioned.

Never had she thought she might be.

And certainly not by this most sexy, gorgeous man, who somehow turned her on with nothing more than a touch.

It startled her how badly she wanted to lift her eyes to his and nod.

For him to take her there.

Wherever 'there' was.

She'd almost forgotten to breathe, Susie realised as she dragged in a long breath. And she wished...oh, she wished she was brave enough to say yes. To just get up from this table and be led to his bed.

Only she'd never been brave in that department.

And, in truth, she didn't really like sex.

At least, she hadn't to date.

'I'm actually working tonight,' she said.

'That's okay.'

'I'd love to, but I do have work, and if I don't give enough notice…'

'Susie.' He smiled, and she wished she could smile so easily when rejected. 'It's fine.'

No, it wasn't fine.

It was Susie who had said no, and yet she was the one fighting not to pout.

'It's not that. I…' What could she say? That she wanted to?

She looked at his eyes, which seemed to draw her to unknown places. She reached for her purse. 'I ought to get going.' She wasn't lying. 'I have to…' She paused and went a little bit pink. 'I'm meeting a friend. Juliet,' she added needlessly. 'And I'm running late.'

He waved away her offer to pay half and she felt his eyes on her as she left.

'Susie!' Mimi was in an absolute panic. 'Dante is here.'

Her violet eyeshadow was bright, but her signature eyeliner was absent, and though she still cut a fabulous dash, she was a little dishevelled.

'*Si?*' Susie said, and pointedly switched to Italian, telling Mimi she had met him last night. She didn't mention she'd just left his table. Oh, and that he'd offered her a night of passionate sex.

'*Avocatto!*'

She frowned, thinking of avocados, and then caught herself and laughed at her own mistranslation—Mimi was bemoaning the fact that he was an attorney.

'He will think I am after Gio's money and the winery. He and Sev will do all they can to dissuade him...'

'Mimi!' Susie slowed down the rather frantic pace. 'Surely the brothers know you're not really his housekeeper?' She looked at probably the most glamorous octogenarian on earth. 'You were an opera singer...'

'A lot of artists fall on hard times.' Mimi sighed. 'Well, that's what we told the boys.'

'Boys?' Susie giggled at Mimi's description of Dante and his older brother, but then checked herself. Mimi really was distressed.

'We told them that when I first moved in,' she said, then halted, her face suddenly brightening.

Susie quickly found out why.

'Dante!' Mimi was suddenly all smiles. *'Buongiorno!'* She switched to English. 'Susie is here.'

'We meet again.' He looked directly at Susie, making her want to squirm.

'I am helping with her Italian,' Mimi told him.

It was Dante who switched to Italian now, asking Mimi if he could speak to her. But of course she was desperate to get away from him and declined, blaming Susie, telling Dante she had paid for an hour-long Italian lesson.

'Ciao!' Mimi said, and hurriedly walked off.

Before Susie could follow there was a brief second when she was alone with Dante.

'Juliet?' He called her out on her lie.

'I should have just said...'

'Did Mimi put you up to helping my grandfather?'

'I'd rather not say...' She could hear Mimi calling for her. 'I'd better go.'

Except she stood, almost as if she was waiting, certainly hoping he might offer dinner again.

He didn't.

'Susie!' Mimi called again.

And she knew she should be relieved that Mimi had dragged her away.

'I cannot believe my bad luck,' Mimi moaned. 'I just hope Gio doesn't tell him about us. I want that ring on my finger before the grandsons interfere.'

'Limited bar menu,' Pedro told the team. 'We are short in the kitchen again.'

Susie felt her jaw grit—and not just in frustration at waitressing.

She should perhaps have been proud of her own restraint, but instead, in the hours that had passed, her regret at declining Dante's offer had increased tenfold.

Perhaps it was for the best, Susie mused now as she waited on tables. She had absolutely nothing suitable to wear for dinner with someone as sophisticated as Dante, and certainly nothing daringly unsuitable in the underwear department...

The thought of one night, no strings, might have appalled her once upon a time—but that was before she met Dante...

Right now, she ached for that one night.

There were a lot of shouts and a lot of laughter in the kitchen. It would seem Cucou was in great spirits tonight. She felt like a cat out in the rain, peering in as she collected some orders.

'Hey, Susie,' called Nico, one of the pastry chefs. 'Cucou said you have a twin.'

'No!' Cucou laughed. 'Not Susie.'

Not Susie.

That should be stencilled on her forehead.

Chiselled on her grave.

Not boring, plain old Susie...

And then everything changed. Or rather, life got interesting.

'Signor Casadio.'

She looked up at Pedro's effusive greeting—he was clearly thrilled to have Gio back in the restaurant. 'We have missed you,' he said to the elderly gentleman, and then he nodded to his stunning companion. *'Signor.'*

'Pedro.' Dante nodded, and then his eyes skimmed past Pedro, and somehow, in a room full of people and noise and all things wonderful, he found her.

Thankfully she didn't have to wait on his table, or the gorgeous pale grey linen shirt he wore might have become the worse for wear.

Instead, she waited on her regular tables, chatting to the guests, trying out her Italian.

She never caught him looking at her, it was absolutely subtle, but she had never felt so aware. She was certain he noted her every move, heard her every word—and then, of course, Gio saw her.

'Susie!' He half stood to greet her. 'It is so good to see you here. So nice to be out.'

'It's lovely to see you too, Gio.' Susie smiled.

'He wanted to go elsewhere.' Gio gestured towards Dante. 'He said I must surely have eaten enough food from Pearla's.'

'Oh!' She smiled, and raised her eyes a fraction. 'That's disappointing to hear.' From the corner of her eye she saw Dante's wry smile at the riposte, aimed at him, then her words were all for Gio. 'Well, we're all thrilled you chose to visit us.'

Should she be disappointed that Dante hadn't wanted to come here tonight?

It didn't feel that way—not in the least.

Perhaps his arrogant pride *had* been a little dented?

She chose to think of it that way, and happily got on with her work.

She was clearing a table of plates, and busy wishing she was doing something else. Shaking a cocktail—or even carrying one. Instead she passed Dante with an armful of crockery.

'Break, Susie,' Pedro said, and she nodded.

'Scusi...'

Dante had put up a hand, and though the table was not her own, she of course had to go over.

'Signor?'

'We'll be getting our coats...'

'Of course.'

'Unless...' he looked to Gio '...you want dessert? Some ice cream, maybe?'

'Please,' Gio dismissed, 'since when did you want dessert?' He looked up to Susie. 'He doesn't even like ice cream.'

'People have been known to change their minds,' Susie said, and smiled at Gio, though again her words were for Dante.

Oh, she hoped he understood what she was trying to convey. But perhaps he didn't get it at all, because he stood glancing at his phone as Pedro helped Gio into his coat.

Then he glanced up and his eyes found hers again.

Oh, gosh.

There was a rush of excitement such as she'd never known. And the searing heat of the kitchen was nothing compared to the heat of his look. She ignited inside.

He was dangerous. He made her feel reckless. How, with one look, did he tell her that she knew so little about her own body?

She'd had just one boyfriend and things had been okay.

Sort of...

Okay... What a pale word. What a pale experience her sex life had been. And now she stood, feeling her body tighten, her breasts full beneath her dress. And low, low in her stomach she felt as if she wore some kind of internal corset that had tightened so much that even the tops of her thighs tensed.

Passion.

He promised passion and she had never known it, Susie realised.

At the end of her shift she stepped out, wondering if he'd understood.

And there he was, holding an ice cream.

'Here,' he said. 'Luckily it is a very cold night.'

'Sour cherry?'

'Of course.'

It was sharp and sweet and utterly her new favourite.

'Did you even try it last night?' she asked.

'No.'

'Try it now.'

But he declined, and they walked down from the walls into the street...where the music from the bars blended with the street performers...and she ought to feel shy, but she was too happy for that.

There were gorgeous sounds coming from the music school as they passed, and she listened to the plucking of a cello.

'My flatmates attend here.'

'Really?'

She nodded, popping the last of her cone into her mouth. 'Their practising drives me mad, but it's so lovely hearing it out here. It makes me want to dance.'

'Then let's dance,' he said, and took her hand.

She hadn't thought their one night might be romantic, and she'd never thought she could feel glamorous in clumpy black shoes, but as she danced under the dark sky the tiny side street was the most romantic, sensual place in the world.

'You make me feel light-footed,' she said, as his face came down to her cheek. 'I can't dance. But...'

'You can,' he told her. 'You can do anything.'

'I haven't done very much at all,' Susie said, and she rather thought they weren't discussing her dancing any more. 'I'm very, very boring…' she warned.

'I don't think so.'

He lowered his head and she stretched to meet his mouth.

This was no awkward first contact.

It came as a relief.

The weight of his mouth on hers felt perfect, and he was heavenly to kiss and to be kissed by. His lips were like velvet, his chin rough, and his body so warm. Closing her eyes at the bliss of his tongue, she tasted him back, and it was both passionate and so good.

His hand slid under her coat and hooked her waist. And then he either pulled her towards him or maybe she just shaped herself into him, as if a mould had been cast.

'I stand corrected,' Dante said. 'I do like sour cherry ice cream.'

He went back for another taste and she clung to his head, kissing him back. The music was silent now. And truly she didn't care if the students were all leaning on the windows and looking out as he kissed her against a wall…

Actually, she did.

Her eyes sprang open. 'I was worried…' she gasped. 'That we were being watched…'

'We're just kissing.'

'Really…?'

She couldn't quite get her breath, and she could feel him hard against her stomach, and she felt swollen herself, just too hot to be out in the cold.

'Come on,' he said, and she nodded as he took her hand and they started to walk.

Still holding her hand, he led her to his house.

They reached Coro Garibaldi… 'How far?' Susie asked as they walked along the elegant avenue.

'Nearly there…'

Except they kept stopping for kisses. And even as they climbed the steps to his door she was impatient. It wasn't just a matter of him taking out his keys, she was almost inside his jacket, trying to find them.

Kissing and laughing, they almost fell inside.

'I'll get the lights,' Dante said.

And that might have been his intention, but first he took off her scarf and hung it over the banister, then he removed her coat and his.

'Let's go to bed,' he suggested.

But she sat on the stairs and removed her horrible shoes and groaned in relief.

'You ache?' he asked.

'I ache,' she agreed, wincing a little as he picked up one foot. 'Please don't.'

She was worried her feet might not be the freshest, but then she stopped caring as he massaged her calf, and then picked up the other foot. And as his fingers dug into her taut calf she found her toes creeping towards his erection.

His hands came to the hem of her dress and slid under it. She lifted her bottom from the stairs and he dealt with her stockings and knickers in one go.

'Bed,' he told her, and stood her up, as if he was ready to carry her if he must.

But then they were kissing again, all traces of sour cherry gone.

'Dante…'

She wanted to explain how unlikely this was, how completely wonderful it was to be too desperate to get to his bed. She was at his belt, feeling him through fabric, and then pulling at his thin jumper. He pulled it over his head and she used her palms to feel his chest. She kissed his flat nipples as he undid her hair.

She liked the semi darkness, but she wanted light to see if his body was as completely magnificent as it felt beneath her hands, or when it was pressed against her. She was almost climbing up him, and he lifted the hem of her dress and gripped his hands onto her bare bottom.

'Please…' Susie said, nervous that this intense feeling might fade on the way to his bedroom, desperate not to lose the new freedom she'd found.

And when he lifted her up, she wrapped her legs around his waist.

Dante was not one for frantic sex in the entrance hall—or, really, frantic sex anywhere. He was always in control. But Susie was light and hot and coiled around him, and clearly they weren't going to make it to bed.

And yet it wasn't frantic…it was slow and delicious, but with a raw edge.

He held her thighs as she wrapped her arms around his neck, and then he lifted her and lowered her onto him. Her breathing was ragged, and she stared at him as he moved her a little, then moaned as he squeezed inside her.

Susie had never had sex standing, and yet she'd never felt further from falling, held in his arms as he moved inside her.

He was so strong, and he held her so securely, that she focussed on the sheer bliss of his thrusts.

Deep and slow.

He sucked her bottom lip and she looked at him with glinting eyes.

'Keep looking at me. Keep looking,' he told her.

And now their eyes were locked, and she felt hot and slick and on the edge of orgasm.

'Dante...'

She wanted to look but her eyes were closing, her neck arching. He was still thrusting, and she felt herself moving, pushing against him, chasing something that had eluded her for ever.

She closed her eyes and just sank into bliss, too selfish to move, pleased that Dante was taking care of that. He was thrusting in and she caught another glimpse of that elusive thing. She clung tighter, and then his sudden shout had it captured. There was a zip of energy, low in her spine, and she let out a cry of delight as he released himself into her.

She felt tender even as it faded.

Still turned on as it ebbed away.

She looked at Dante and smiled. 'I've never managed that before.'

He stared.

'I've always...' She stopped.

'Faked it?'

She nodded.

'Let's go upstairs.'

CHAPTER FOUR

Susie woke with her face buried in the side of Dante's chest, and it took her a moment to work out not so much where she was, but how they'd made it to his bed.

He'd carried her.

All limp and sated from her first orgasm.

He had carried her here, and then they'd done it again.

With Susie on top.

Gosh.

She rolled onto her back and saw stars. Literally. His ceiling was an artwork of stars and moons and angels and just so many beautiful things that she thought she could stare for ever as she remembered last night.

And then what had mattered little last night suddenly mattered a lot, and she screwed her eyes closed.

Oh, God. They hadn't used anything.

'I know.' His deep voice answered her frantic thoughts and she turned anxious eyes towards him. 'Common sense seems to have eluded us both last night.'

'I can't believe it,' she groaned. 'I mean...' She had known they were unprotected, and so had he! 'I'm usually so careful.'

'You said you were on the pill.'

That's right...

Somewhere before their second time they'd both rather feebly addressed the matter.

'I am.'

Susie nodded. She was more cross with herself than him. Or simply stunned that she, Susie Bilton, could so completely lose her head.

'Then we have nothing to worry about. I've never had unprotected sex.' Perhaps he saw the doubt creep into her eyes, because he added, 'Susie, last night really was an anomaly.' He seemed to consider. 'Maybe it's because...' His voice trailed off as he attempted to rationalise what had occurred. 'The change in routine.' He turned and gave a slow, triumphant smile. 'That must be it.'

'That is the most ridiculous excuse ever,' she chided lightly. 'So, I'm a change in routine?'

'You are.'

'I'm not sure I want to know your usual routine.'

He gave a soft laugh. 'I meant I've never brought a lover here...'

'Never?'

'Absolutely not—you saw what that waiter was like this morning...way too interested...'

'It was lovely, though, wasn't it?' Susie said.

'Very,' Dante agreed, although he didn't tend to discuss such events afterwards.

He was about to climb from the bed. Do his usual and offer coffee, to be polite, in the hope that she'd say no. Especially as—bonus—he didn't have any milk.

It didn't feel like a bonus, though.

The bonus was her wide-eyed smile.

'Twice,' she said, and took a happy breath.

Yet still he lay there.

Usually Dante loathed morning conversation, and he had sometimes wondered if he was the only guy on earth who didn't particularly like morning sex.

Well, he liked the sex part... Just not feeling like a louse afterwards, for wanting her gone.

But this morning he wanted to prolong the conversation. He looked over at the woman in his bed and did not want her gone.

She was looking up at the art on his ceiling. 'It's gorgeous,' she said. 'So much detail.'

He joined her looking skywards. 'It was beneath plaster when I bought the house. The previous owner gave up on a full restoration and concealed it. The dining room has one too.'

'Gosh...'

'I found someone in Florence to restore it.'

He had admired it at the time, and on occasions since, but his times here were brief, and generally fraught with memories as he was often here attending memorials. Even celebrations like Christmas made Gio morose and, of course, at times, there was the strain of himself and Sev putting on a front, pretending they still had a relationship...

No, he'd never really taken the time to appreciate what was before his eyes, where planets and stars fought in a deep crimson sky.

But there was a little frown on her face. Perhaps she was still cross about their carelessness last night?

'So,' Dante said. 'What's your excuse?'

'Hmmm?'

'For last night.'

What *was* her excuse? Susie thought, and was quiet for a moment as she lay pondering his question.

'I don't have one,' she finally admitted, and saw him turn to the sound of her quiet bemusement. 'I don't know.'

She wasn't being evasive—she simply didn't know how to describe what had happened to her.

'I've never forgotten myself like that,' she admitted.

'Forgotten yourself?' he checked.

She didn't know how better to describe it, but there had been the light stroke of his fingers on her stomach and then...

She'd had one relationship and so little to compare...

'I just lost my head,' Susie said, and she even tried a little joke. 'Too much ice cream!'

'Do you want coffee?' he asked.

'I do.'

As he rolled from the bed and dressed, she looked at his stunning long legs and taut bottom, and watched as he pulled on some clothes. Gosh, she wanted him to climb back into bed.

'Are you leaving me here?'

'I'm getting us coffee. I didn't let anyone know I was coming.'

'Anyone?' she checked,

'I have a housekeeper. I would usually let her know when I'm staying.'

'Your home's stunning.' She looked at the bold red walls. 'It's incredible. Just...'

Susie didn't quite know what else to say. It was like something out of a lifestyle magazine. But for all that it was lavish, there was nothing here that spoke of *him*. She looked at the ornate wardrobes and for a brief second wondered if there were even any clothes in them.

She let the conversation die, happy to watch as he raked his fingers through his hair to comb it and ran a hand over his unshaven jaw.

'How do you have your coffee?' he asked.

'Lots of milk.'

'I shan't be long.'

It was a little awkward. She lay there silent, but managed a half-smile as he let himself out, then lay there some more and waited for the cringe of utter regret to spike now that she was alone.

Except...there was none.

Now the conversation had been had as to their reckless-ness, there was none.

She didn't regret last night at all.

It had been a complete revelation.

A small part of her had thought that deep longing and fe-vered want didn't exist for her.

Hauling herself from his delicious bed, she made her way to the bathroom. It was all marble and gold taps. No stars on the ceilings, though, but still decadent.

Bathed and smelling gorgeous, from all his lovely soaps and such, she wrapped herself in a huge towel and stared into the full-length mirror that leant on the bathroom wall... She tried to think of practical things, like where she'd left her clothes.

And although she would have loved to climb back into the high, rumpled bed, she pinched his comb instead.

Back in the bedroom, her eyes were drawn to a thick golden card. She couldn't help but peek—and then was startled when she got caught...

Dante stood at the door and informed her about what she was reading. 'The Lucca Spring Ball.'

'Yes. It looks incredible. Mimi's told me about it.'

She turned and saw that he had brought up not just coffee but her clothes. It really was time to leave, Susie realised as she replaced the thick card.

'Sorry...' She took the coffee from him and truly didn't know how they should be together. 'I wasn't angling for you to invite me.'

'I would hope not,' he commented as he moved to lie side-ways on the bed and watch her dress. 'Given it's six weeks away.'

'And we're just for one night.' She'd got the message and wanted him to know that she had. 'Anyway, it's my birthday that weekend.'

'How old will you be?'

'Twenty-five—and my parents are coming.'

'Is that nice?'

'Very.' She smiled as she clipped on her bra. 'I can't wait to have them here on my birthday.' She separated her knickers from her tights, wishing there was a more elegant way to do things. 'And have them all to myself.'

'All to yourself?'

'On my birthday.' She knew she sounded petty and jealous—possibly she was—so she shook her head and smiled. 'What are you doing today?'

'I'll check in on Gio...see if I can get him to talk. We're not brilliant at it.'

'How come?' she asked. 'I mean, you're very direct.'

'Do you talk easily with *your* family about difficult topics?'

'No,' Susie admitted. 'I just...' She slipped on her dress and sat on the bed to do up the zip at the back.

He watched her wrestle.

It was by far safer.

Dante was conflicted. He wanted her gone and yet he wanted her back in his bed—and the latter did not sit well for him.

Last night had perturbed him, and his continued desire for her this morning was doing the same.

'I'm not very good at this,' she admitted suddenly, and he felt a twist inside at the tense rise in her voice. 'I mean, I don't know how I should be...'

'It's okay,' he said, and gave in on not helping. Sitting up, he dealt with her zip, and then he held her hips for a moment, with her back to him. 'It was a great night.'

'Yes...'

'I leave for Milan this evening.'

'I know that.'

'I have to go and see Gio,' he said, as if reminding himself there was a reason he should not prolong this encounter. 'Sort out all the old jewellery. It's a job he has been putting off for a long time.'

'Yes.' She nodded. 'I'm sure it will be difficult.'

'He gets upset...'

'I meant...' She swallowed. 'It will be difficult for both of you.' She let out a breath. 'They're not just his wife's jewels...' she ventured. 'There's your mother's jewellery too.' She didn't turn her head. 'He showed me some.'

'Yes,' said Dante, rather pleased that her back was still to him, and a little stunned to hear his silent dread about today being acknowledged. 'He has most of it.'

'Most? Do you have some?'

Her enquiry, Dante thought, was gentle. And it was a natural question, an invitation to ask if he'd kept some sentimental pieces. But when he'd said 'most' that wasn't what he'd meant.

He briefly thought of the small stones in his safe in Milan, but it was by far too painful to go there.

Even in his own head.

And if ever one day he did, then he would be alone.

Ensuring the agony was wiped from his features, he turned her around within the circle of his hands, her hips beneath his palms, and looked up at her damp blonde hair and pale face.

Why were they ending things here? Dante asked himself.

'I'd better go,' Susie said. 'I have homework...'

Her voice was a little strained and high.

'What's your homework?' he asked.

'Greetings, thanks and farewells.' She smiled at him. 'How do I say *Thank you for last night*?'

'Try,' he told her.

'Grazie per la scorsa notte?'

Dante gave in.

'I could help you with your homework.'

'Really?'

'Stay?'

He saw Susie tense as he said the word, as if her body was warning her...

'I have to go and visit the winery,' he told her, and then he looked up at her blue eyes. She was uncertain whether to stay, and that helped—because he was uncertain if he should have asked. 'It's not exactly fun—I have to speak with the manager and such—but we could get lunch?'

'I'd like that.' Susie nodded.

He pulled her down onto his knee. 'You'll have to try and keep your hands off me, or Gio and Mimi will find out.'

'I'm sure I can manage.'

She felt shiny with pleasure—not just because this wasn't goodbye, it was the way he made her feel.

'I'm not so sure I'll be able to,' he told her, and they shared a slow kiss, his jaw rough and his tongue exquisite. And it was so much nicer to kiss than to say goodbye.

'You have to go to Gio's,' she reminded him as his hands moved her dress up.

He turned her around so she straddled his lap.

'I know I do,' he said, with both a smile and a dash of regret.

But even as he went to tip her from his lap she resisted. Not demanding more kisses...she had something to say.

'Talk to Gio about the jewellery...'

'Sorry?'

'You said it was difficult to get him to open up. I think talking about the jewellery with him might help...'

'We've already spoken about it. I told him I would take it to Milan.' He halted, recalling the conversation. Gio had been talking and he had shut it down.

The jewellery was a painful topic for Dante.

For all of them.

'Okay,' Dante said. 'I'll give it a try.'

Now Susie stood. 'I ought to pop back home…' She gestured to her dress. 'Get a change of clothes.'

Then she thought of another rather essential matter—her pills, sitting in her bedside drawer.

'Meet back here?' he checked.

She nodded.

'I'll order a driver.'

'Pick me up if it's easier.'

'I've got a lockbox,' he said. 'I'll give you the code. Just let yourself in whenever.'

'You're sure?' she checked.

And no, he wasn't sure—because Dante did not give out such information, or have people in his space without him. And yet all his rules seemed to be falling by the wayside.

This was more than he'd expected, or perhaps even wanted, but it was hard to let go of bliss, hard to shut the door on such a delicious reprieve.

'Meet back here,' he affirmed.

Juliet and Louanna were both practising. Susie could hear the violin and the cello as she climbed the stairs to her apartment.

She went in quietly and headed straight for her bedroom.

Staring into the large wooden wardrobe, she looked at the clothes she had hanging there. A pair of jeans, a spare uniform. Some rather boring jumpers and a couple of thick skirts that she wore with boots.

Certainly nothing that matched her mood.

And her mood was…

She examined her feelings for a moment, as if reaching in and feeling the touchstone of her soul, and knew she was happy. Exhilarated…

Grabbing her toiletries bag, she went and brushed her teeth and then reached for her pills.

Today was Sunday…

So why were Friday and Saturday still in their tiny igloos? *Today*, she said to herself, *is definitely Sunday.*

And it would seem her brain had ceased being sensible on Friday.

The moment Dante had stepped into her life.

'Breathe,' Susie told herself aloud. 'It will be fine.'

She changed into fresh clothes—jeans and a lilac jumper—and then Louanna called out.

'Are you up?'

'Yes,' Susie said, realising as she headed out to the lounge that they hadn't noticed she'd been gone all night.

'You look nice.' Juliet smiled. 'Are you on your way out?'

'Yes, I'm going to a winery.' Susie nodded. 'With a friend.'

'You should try De Santis,' Louanna suggested. 'For cheap wine, it's pretty good.'

'We were thinking of Casadio.'

'Hah!' Louanna said. She rolled her eyes and offered an Italian saying. *'Costare una fortuna…'* A warning that she would pay a very high price.

'I'll keep it in mind.'

'You're not going to the restaurant there, are you?' Louanna checked, running her eyes over Susie's jeans. 'It's very elegant.'

'She looks lovely,' Juliet jumped in.

'I'm just saying…' Louanna shrugged. 'I'd want someone to tell *me* if I wasn't suitably dressed.'

'Thanks, I think!' Susie said, smiling to Juliet, who rolled her gorgeous green eyes. 'I'd better go shopping…'

There was steady rain, so the shops were quiet. She looked in the beautifully dressed boutique windows, but it was all a bit intimidating.

Susie wasn't offended by what Louanna had said—well, a touch, maybe—and she did appreciate the heads-up. More than that, it had been for ever since she'd shopped for something nice to wear. She'd been saving for her trip, and before that...

She thought of her ex, who hadn't ever seemed to notice when she'd gone all out, so in the end she hadn't bothered.

Everyone had been surprised that she'd ended things between them—even Susie had struggled to justify it to herself. The relationship hadn't been awful, or terrible, or any of those things, but she had suddenly seen how she'd hidden her true self. She had wanted to be more adventurous—not just in bed, but in everything. But she'd stuffed down the little hurts rather than voice them.

Passing the ice-cream shop, she thought of Dante waiting outside the restaurant with a cone.

She didn't quite get how a simple thing like an ice cream could mean so much.

Was it that he'd thought of her when she wasn't there? Queued up to get the treat because he knew it was something she liked? That he'd known she secretly wanted that flavour... that he'd noticed.

He made her feel noticed. And even if this was very temporary, it was thrilling, and an adventure, and under his delicious attention she was discovering herself.

She ventured into one of the shops, but she had no real idea what she was looking for.

'For lunch where?'

The assistant who had offered to help nodded when she said she was going to a winery in the Tuscan hills.

'Perhaps these?'

She held up some gorgeous black jeans, but then pulled them back when Susie explained that it was Casadio.

'The cellar door, or the restaurant?'

'I think...' She had no idea. 'I don't know...possibly the restaurant?'

'Hmm...' The assistant clearly considered this a conundrum. 'Okay,' she said, heading over to a small rack that sadly wasn't a discount one. 'You can dress these up, or...'

She held up a grey woollen dress, but Susie's eyes had lit on another.

It was the palest blue and the softest wool, and if she was going to splurge for the first time, then... She took a breath. She might as well adore her purchase.

The wool was thin and soft, yet snug, and the neckline was a little scooped, but not too low. There was a thick belt in the same wool, but that dressed it down too much.

'Look.' The assistant showed her a gold belt and looped it round her hips. 'With stilettoes, you could even go to a party.'

'Yes.' She laughed. 'But I don't really go to many parties.' Sometimes she was a waitress at them...

But yes, absolutely this could work for a glamorous party. And for lunch with Dante.

'I love it.' Susie nodded.

And she loved the pretty underwear she bought too.

Arriving back at his place, she found the key in his lockbox and stepped into his gorgeous home, hiding the bags because she didn't want him to know the effort she had gone to.

She looked around the kitchen at the gorgeous copper pots, the huge ovens that could cater for a small party, the wooden bench... There was even a little herb garden in the window, and yet from all he'd told her he was rarely here.

She walked through the hall and into a lounge. The walls were a silky navy and there were beams that ran across the high ceilings. Every room was a masterpiece. It was like viewing a stately home, Susie thought, as she peered into a beautiful dining room.

Yet there was nothing of *him*.

No photos, no mementoes.

She went back to the kitchen. He didn't even have one fridge magnet.

Susie collected them wherever she went. Possibly it was one of her many weaknesses.

It unnerved her a little that his house, while stunning, was so impersonal, and it reminded her that Dante got attached to no one. It would be wise to keep an emotional distance.

Yes, the sex was incredible, and he was too, but to get too close to Dante could seriously hurt.

CHAPTER FIVE

DANTE WASN'T CLOSE to anyone—though he did make an effort for Gio.

'Hey...' He gave him a kiss. 'Is there anything you want me to discuss with Christo at the winery?'

'No, just make sure he is happy...ask if there's anything he needs.'

'Of course. I spoke to him last week.'

'Face to face is better, Dante.'

'I know.' He took a breath. 'So, you want to get these cleaned?' He took a seat and picked up one of the bracelets. 'This was Nonna's, yes?'

'No.' Gio shook his head. 'That was my grandmother's.' He looked at the sapphires, then paused as Dante picked up a string of pearls. 'They were your mother's.'

'Yes.' Dante nodded, assailed by memories of her and his papa about to head out. He put them back down, instead lifted a heavy emerald choker. 'This was Nonna's?'

'There's a stone loose,' Gio said. 'I should have had it looked at ages ago. She liked them to be cleaned at least every year.'

'We'll sort it.'

'When?'

'I can call the jeweller...' He paused, thought of his hectic week, but decided, for Gio, he would take some time off. 'I could see if we can go in tomorrow.'

'Tomorrow?' Gio sounded a little panicked. 'We'll do this tomorrow?'

'If you want.' Dante nodded, and was reaching for some rather awful earrings when his grandfather finally stated his truth.

'Mimi is not my housekeeper.'

'Okay...' Dante said, picking up the awful earrings.

'She never was my housekeeper.'

'Mimi makes you happy?'

'So happy,' Gio said. 'And I make her happy too. After her Eric died she cried for two years, and I understand that. When I lost your *nonna* I thought my life was over, and then the accident... I never thought I would be truly happy again. But when Mimi sings...' He wiped his eyes. 'Sometimes she looks at me and sings and my heart soars again.'

'If you make each other so happy, why isn't she here?'

'Mimi wants to make things official.'

'I see.'

'And I have to sort all these first,' Gio said. 'Take care of the past that I've been neglecting. I don't want to be sad and lonely. I want to hold Mimi's hand on my morning walk.'

'Then do it,' Dante said, and gave Gio a hug. 'Make it official.'

Gio mopped his eyes. 'It's time to be happy, Dante. To move on from the past.'

'Yes.'

'Not just me.'

'Gio, I have moved on. Don't worry about me.' Dante was practical. 'We'll get the jewels sorted. I'll come with you.'

'I was going to use this central stone for her ring.' Gio picked up a ruby bracelet. 'The stone is so beautiful...and rubies are very romantic.'

Dante didn't care for rubies. He had two in his safe that no one knew about... He pushed that thought aside. 'Perfect.'

'I thought so too.' He was suddenly defeated. 'However, Susie said no.'

Dante frowned. For a second he wondered if he'd given himself away by reacting to Susie's name.

'She said I should get a new stone for Mimi—something I chose myself, that is just for her.'

'Why?' Dante asked, and he wasn't just being his usual unromantic self. It was because he was happier to pursue the conversation when the topic was Susie. 'You have more jewels than you know what to do with. I am sure Mimi would love this.'

'I said the same. The ruby is spectacular. But Susie seems to think Mimi would want a new stone.'

'It wasn't Nonna's,' Dante pointed out, but he saw Gio flinch, and knew it was still a delicate matter for him. 'It's a beautiful ruby…it's been in your family for years.'

'Yes.' Gio nodded. 'That's what I thought. I was going use the gold from the chain I used to wear when I was younger, but Susie said even the gold should be new.'

'New?' Dante frowned. 'When it's melted down gold is gold.'

His grandfather gave a low laugh at his wry response. 'I said the same, but I'd invited her opinion and she suggested I choose something new and special, just for Mimi.'

'It's a ring, Gio. I don't know what Susie's going on about.'

'Susie has twin sisters,' Gio told him, and then added, 'Identical.'

'And…?'

'They're very close in age—just a little over a year older than Susie is.'

'And?' Dante said again, a little perplexed as to what that had to do with anything, but curious. 'Is one of them a master jeweller?'

'No.' Gio laughed, and Dante was pleased to see the sparkle

in Gio's eyes had returned. 'Susie was always getting things handed down to her. Clothes, toys…'

'That's hardly the same as jewellery.'

'She seems to think so. Apparently, she always felt left out—their birthdays were always grouped together, and their presents were similar. I have to make this just about Mimi.'

'Mimi's not a twin, and she doesn't have any sisters who are twins…' Dante didn't get it.

'No, but she is unique.'

And then Dante got it a little bit more. Susie ached to be the talk of the town, for attention, for the spotlight to shine briefly on her, to stand out rather than fade into the background. And he felt a twisting ache in the black hole that existed where his heart had once been.

'Yes,' Dante agreed. 'She is.'

And he wasn't really talking about Mimi—he was thinking about Susie, and how he was now determined to make this day a little special.

Susie was ready on time, and when a dark car slid up outside she wondered if perhaps she was meeting Dante there.

She slipped on her coat and was just tying up her scarf when Dante came rushing through the door.

'Two minutes,' he said.

'How was Gio?'

'Come up,' he said, stripping off and dashing into the shower. 'Talking about the jewellery helped.'

'Good.'

She sat on the edge of the bath, enjoying watching him quickly wash, then frowning when he dashed out and lathered his chin to shave.

'I thought we were in a rush.'

'We are.'

'It can't be that much of a rush,' Susie said, 'if you've time to shave.'

'Call an ambulance if ever I don't,' he teased, wiping his jaw and then pulling on a black shirt.

Within a matter of moments he was back to looking like a *Vogue* model, elegant and polished, and soon they were headed out to the car.

'It's not fair,' she grumbled as they sat inside.

'What isn't?'

'How lovely you look in so little time.'

'You look lovely, too,' Dante said, looking at the mascara on her lashes, her glossy lips, her hair freshly brushed and worn down. 'You've really helped with Gio.'

'What happened?'

'I'll tell you when we're there.'

'I can't wait.'

But for now it was nice to simply relax as the car took them out of town and into the gorgeous countryside. Dante showed her fields that in summer were a blaze of yellow, filled with sunflowers. Then the car slowed down as it climbed the hills and they passed a church that was somehow familiar.

Then she knew why. She recognised it from one of the many photos Gio had shown her. It was the church where Sev had married.

She glanced at Dante, who was going through the messages on his phone.

'Is this it?' she asked, as a sign for a winery came up, rustic and pretty and very Tuscan. 'It's gorgeous.'

'That's not it,' he said, with an edge to his low voice. 'That's the De Santis winery.'

'Oh, I've heard it's good. Well, for cheap wine...'

'It's like vinegar,' he said. 'Always rushed through. It's Sev's wife's...or rather his late wife's family winery,' he explained, and there was still that edge to his voice.

'Rose?'

'Rosa,' he corrected, and it was as though he had to keep his mouth from curling with distaste just saying her name.

Susie knew there was a lot of tension around the wedding.

Looking out at the grey rolling clouds, she tried to remember who had told her what. Mimi had told her on their walks about Sev and Rosa's wedding in the beautiful little church, and the tragedy of the funeral just a few months later. Gio, too, had shown her photos of his gorgeous family outside the church.

Susie hadn't known Dante then—but she'd seen his cut and black eye.

'We're here,' Dante said.

Unlike the De Santis winery, Casadio's wasn't quaint or rustic. The dark signage was sophisticated, the driveway long, and clearly it was a slick operation.

Dante parked, and as she climbed out Susie saw there was a large shop. Then they walked around the side, and spread before them was a hillside full of vines and a gorgeous outdoor area with tables.

'Dante.' A gentleman came out, all smiles, and greeted him effusively.

'Susie, this is Christos.' Dante introduced him. 'Our manager.'

Christos led them up to a gorgeous restaurant that was every bit as luxurious as Pearla's, yet very relaxed and spread out. He spoke in rapid Italian, but thankfully Dante translated easily.

'He's asking if you would like a tour while we talk, or to relax on the couches?'

'Oh.' She looked at the huge roaring fire and as she took off her scarf she opted for the couches. 'The couches sound lovely.'

'We shouldn't be too…' Dante started, but as she slipped off her coat he found out what it meant to be lost for words.

He'd only seen her in her waitressing dress, or naked in his bed, or wrapped in a sheet, and he was momentarily stunned. Her dress was the colour of the sky in spring, and it was somehow demure and sexy as hell all at once.

Or was it sexy because he knew what lay beneath?

Everyone else seemed unperturbed. Christos's wife was taking her coat, Christos himself was guiding her to the couches. So Dante, refusing to react like some awkward teenager at a party, went over to the bar, turned his back on her and chatted to the bar manager.

He would really rather have joined Susie on the couches, but instead he walked through the cellars with Christos. Then he met with the vigneron and listened to all he had to say. Then Christos suggested they walk through the vines.

Being shown through a place where he had once played hide and seek, where he had run, where he'd once had a happy family, was hell.

He liked Christos—he just did not want to be playing owner today.

Especially when he had the intriguing Susie waiting.

Oh, she was so far from predictable…

She was sitting on a huge leather sofa, gazing out at the view that he saw only in nightmares, with a vague smile on her face.

'Susie?' He interrupted her wherever her daydreams had taken her. 'Do you want to eat?'

'Yes!' She didn't stand, though. 'I was talking to the chef, and he said we could do a tasting here. They'll bring all the foods and wine over.'

'A tasting?' he checked. 'They'll explain all the wines, all the food…'

'Yes.'

'Why don't we just get a table and eat? A tasting is very…'

'Sociable?' She laughed.

'Yes,' he said, sitting down beside her with a sigh. 'Okay we'll do a tasting.'

He signalled to a waiter and told him to go ahead, but when they were alone again he turned to her.

'Before they start, I'm going to tell you something.'

'Okay…'

'No one else knows this…' He cupped his hand and whispered in her ear. 'I don't actually like wine.'

'Seriously?'

He pulled his head back and nodded. 'Why do you think I went to study law?'

'Are you telling the truth?'

'I can drink it. And at family events and functions here, or events that we sponsor, I do. But…' He rolled his eyes. 'I might as well be drinking cheap De Santis wine; it all tastes the same to me.'

'Does it?'

'Almost.' He gave her a smile. 'De Santis is exceptionally bad. Still, I don't really get it. It is all Gio talks about—and Christos. Sev knows his stuff too. So do you…'

'I don't.'

'"A Sauvignon will pair nicely…"' he quoted her, teasing. 'I'm playing…' He gave her a smile and looked down at her dress. 'You look stunning.'

'Thank you.'

'You do,' he told her. 'I feel like they just opened my case at customs…'

'I don't understand what you're saying…'

'Unexpected goods inside.'

She started to laugh.

'Seriously, I am here on a sort of business lunch, and all I want is to make out with you on the sofa…'

'Better not,' Susie said. 'It'll get straight back to Gio.'

* * *

It was fun.

Even if Dante didn't much like wine.

Possibly *because* Dante didn't much like wine!

It made her smile as he listened intently and swirled his drink. Susie just sipped it.

'Yum,' she said about the 'peppery red with a hint of blackcurrant', as described by their server. 'It is peppery.'

'Yes...' Dante joined in her little joke. 'With a hint of blackcurrant.'

And there was more 'yum' as she ate thick olives and gorgeous meats and cheeses from this very beautiful land.

'Wait...' Dante said, and then he trickled truffled honey over some cheese. 'Now try it.'

Susie closed her eyes as she tasted it. 'Oh, my goodness...' It was incredible. 'I have to get some to take home.'

It was a lovely, long lunch, and finally they were on the dessert wine, and Christos was explaining to them what they were tasting in great and long detail.

'I like this one,' Susie said. 'I might get some.'

Finally the tasting was over and the social side done, and they both sat back on the couch and smiled at each other.

'That was actually good,' Dante said.

'It was. I might bring my parents here when they visit.'

'Do,' Dante said. 'Speak to Christos when you book.'

'You can pay for my lunch today,' Susie said. 'But not my parents'.'

Susie intrigued him.

As Gio had said, she was delightful. He found her forthright, but at times shy, and very kind.

But there was so much more to her. Little bits of which he had found out today.

He wanted her to tell him more herself.

* * *

'Are you going to tell me about Gio?' Susie asked, surprised she'd waited so long to ask. They'd been enjoying each other so much...

'He told me that he was in love with Mimi.'

Susie smiled, utterly thrilled that Gio had finally told his grandson, as well as curious to know how Dante had taken it.

'How do you feel about it?'

'Feel?' He paused with his glass on its way to his lips. 'Relieved that he's told me and very pleased that he's been talking to you. How did you get him to talk?'

'He was quite...' She hesitated. 'I was worried the first night I took a meal over to him.'

'Was he upset?'

'No...' Susie thought back. 'I think *determined* better describes his mood then. He didn't tell me anything then—just said that he had all the numbers he needed in his phone.'

'My fault.' Dante rolled his eyes. 'I gave him a few lessons on how to use it and put a few numbers in...like Pearla's...'

'He wasn't so great the next night,' Susie told him. 'He started to talk about his late wife, and how marriage is sacred. He showed me a few photos.' Susie smiled. 'I came out and Mimi was waiting for me. I didn't know who she was, of course.'

It was nice to be able to tell Dante now.

'She was beside herself, but determined to stand her ground. She asked if I could do a few things for him—without Gio knowing, of course.'

'How did you sort out the furniture? He told me you moved it yourself.'

'No!' Susie laughed. 'I took him for a walk and while we were out Cucou and Pedro came, with a few of the pastry chefs. They've been really looking out for him—discreetly, of course. He's very loved.'

'Yes, and he and Cucou go way back. They have been friends for ever.'

'How do you feel about it?' Susie asked again, thinking of Mimi's doom and gloom predictions where Dante was concerned. Although he really didn't seem bothered. Or perhaps they weren't close enough to discuss such things as his grandfather's estate? 'Do you have any concerns?'

'I had concerns when I found out he was alone in that vast house,' Dante said. 'But I'm pleased for him. God knows, he's been through it…'

So had Dante, Susie thought, yet he spoke only about Gio's pain.

'He says it's time for him to be happy, to move on from the past, and I want that for him. He didn't deserve what happened.'

'Nobody deserves that,' Susie said, and frowned when Dante didn't answer. 'Nobody.'

'I know,' Dante responded.

He didn't sound entirely convinced.

Surely he didn't blame himself?

He'd never spoken about the accident, though, and she wasn't sure it was her place to ask, or even how she'd do it, and so, instead of delving, she asked about his brother.

'Does Sev know about Gio and Mimi?'

'He's going to call him today.'

'You haven't told him?'

'No,' he admitted.

'Did he have his suspicions too? About them being a couple?'

'Probably—he's very sharp.'

'But the two of you have never discussed it?'

'We don't really talk about things like that.'

'Like what?'

'We don't talk about much,' Dante said. 'Just how Gio is, and the business side of things.'

And perhaps she oughtn't delve—they were nibbling little chocolates and drinking dessert wine, and according to the rules they were together for a good time, not a long time—but Susie found she couldn't quite let things go.

'Were you ever close?' she asked.

'Yeah.' He nodded, but didn't elaborate. Instead he asked her a question. 'Are you close?' he asked. 'With your siblings?'

'I guess…' Susie started. But, given she wanted to know more about Dante, it felt wrong to hide part of herself, and so she shook her head. 'We're not as close as I'd like to be. My sisters are inseparable: they work together, have their own little chat group, and they'll be living together soon. I found out yesterday that they're getting a flat together. By accident,' she added. 'They haven't actually told me yet.'

'So how do you know?'

'They sent a text that wasn't meant for me…' She could feel her heart sink just as it had when she'd received it—just as it did whenever she felt pushed away or excluded. 'It was quickly deleted, but I'd already seen it.'

'Damn phones,' he said, and gave her a gentle smile. 'I hear it happens all the time—not that that helps.'

'It actually does help,' Susie corrected. 'It's not like discovering an affair, or anything, but I knew it wasn't meant for me and it hurt.' She took a breath. 'They're twins…'

'Gio mentioned that,' Dante told her. 'So, you feel left out?'

'Not just left out. I was never let in.'

She could feel tears stinging her eyes, but hoped she could blame the low afternoon sun streaming through the glass. She was certain she sounded pathetic—especially to someone who had lost so much. Yet he was the first person she'd ever really opened up to…the first person who had insisted she be herself.

'They'll tell me when they're ready.' She shrugged. 'I'm pleased for them, really.'

'Liar.' He smiled as he called her out. And then he gave her something to think about. 'Would you want to share a flat with them?'

'No!' She gave a half-laugh, but it soon faded. 'It would be nice to be asked, though.' She sighed. 'I must sound very jealous.'

'Are you?'

'Of course not.' She shook her head, possibly a little too quickly. 'My mother often accuses me of being so, but...' She decided she didn't want to be *that* honest! 'I do love them. They're great, honestly. And they're gorgeous.'

'So are you.'

'No, they're seriously beautiful—they turn heads wherever they go.'

Dante listened to her denial, and even as she lied to his face, still she made him smile. She was so jealous. He could feel it—could see it choking her as she spoke. And he adored her for it. Adored how she tried so hard to speak nicely of people... how she insisted everything was perfectly fine.

'Why are you smiling?' Susie asked, a little bemused by his expression.

'You turn heads.'

'Stop it,' she said, feeling his eyes on her mouth and aching to kiss him.

'I could very easily make you the talk of the town,' Dante told her, looking at her lips, still glossy with truffled honey. 'I could kiss you here.'

'Perhaps not,' Susie said, not feeling quite so brave at the prospect of people knowing about her fling with Dante.

And it wasn't because she'd be embarrassed—it was more

that she could glimpse Monday, and Tuesday, and all the days afterwards, possibly having to laugh it off to Louanna, or whoever, after he'd gone. The pastry chefs, too, were always delighted to gossip…

She saw it again—that glimpse of having to shrug it off. Pretend it didn't really matter.

She looked into brown eyes that seemed to be just waiting for them to be alone, and she blushed pink in the face of such blatant desire, feeling warm in her dress, and in the heat of his gaze, and she simply didn't know how a Sunday could be more perfect…

'Do you want to go back?' Dante asked, with a purr of suggestion. 'Examine those unexpected goods?'

'I do.' Susie nodded. 'But…'

Yes, she did want to go back, and discover herself with him. To do some more of the things she'd missed out on. And yet she knew, or rather guessed, that this place must be agony for Dante. There was a darkness to him here, a pain that felt almost palpable at times. Or perhaps she recognised the loneliness she so often felt. Having no one to really talk to—even if in Dante's case it was by choice.

'It's so nice…sitting here talking. Or aren't your temporary lovers supposed to say that?'

'I told you,' Dante said, 'you can say whatever you want. You're not used to that?'

'Meaning?'

'You don't often speak up?'

'Perhaps…' Susie admitted. 'Okay, then.' She would speak up. 'I'd like to stay here a bit longer. What time do you fly?'

'Damn!' he said, and sat up quickly. And then he saw she was startled. 'It's okay, I'm not panicking at the prospect of more conversation. I have to let my pilot know.' He took out his phone. 'The helicopter is booked for this evening.'

'Helicopter?' She frowned as his call was swiftly dealt with. 'You surely don't...?' She halted. 'Sorry.'

'For what? You think I should be avoiding helicopters, given what happened?'

And, while she was all for speaking up, Susie knew this might have crossed the line. 'I shouldn't have said anything.'

'There's only one commercial flight a day from Milan to here,' he said. 'And I am not chartering a whole plane just for that. As Gio would say, we have to think of the planet!'

'Doesn't it scare you?'

'No.' He shook his head. 'I flew on a helicopter straight after I heard about the accident. I just wanted to get back to Gio.'

Her hands met his and touched the tip of his fingers. 'I'm so sorry.'

'It was a long time ago,' Dante said, and then he looked to the window, and the grey, heavy skies that must be so unlike that clear, bright day. 'I could see the smoke as we flew over...' He pointed to the hills. 'Right there—just where the snow caps the middle one. A little way up...'

'You saw it?'

'I can still see it,' he admitted.

'So you hate coming home?'

'I do,' he agreed. 'Though not so much this time.'

He gave her hand a squeeze, and it was Susie who wanted to pull back.

He'd said it so nicely, yet she couldn't help but feel like a diversion. A little respite from the pain of his past. But then who could blame him for that? And wasn't he a little respite for her? A boost to her confidence? Someone she felt brave enough to try new things with, to discover her body with and soothe her wants with his skilful hands?

Yet right now it wasn't just sex. Only the tips of their fingers were still touching...

* * *

Dante had never spoken about it—not really, but Gio had got to him. He'd seen the doubt in his grandfather's eyes when he'd insisted to him that he'd moved on.

He had.

Surely he had?

Yet aside from practical reasons he'd never told anyone about that day. Oh, he'd listened to Gio endlessly go on, accepted condolences, but he'd never talked about it.

Possibly to prove to himself that he could, he decided to tell Susie.

Susie—whom he'd never see again after this day.

'My parents were coming to Milan to visit me. They were taking me for lunch…they wanted to talk. To be honest, I wasn't looking forward to it. I'd just finished university and was starting an internship in Milan.'

'They wanted you back here in Lucca?'

'In part. But I think it was more to discuss why Sev and I were not talking. We'd had an argument a few months before that.'

Susie nodded. 'Gio showed me the wedding photo.'

'Yeah…' He gave a resigned half-laugh. 'I'm not getting into that, but…'

She saw Dante reach for the wine he didn't much like and take a sip, then put down his glass.

Then she felt his fingers come back to her own. And even if neither was really one for holding hands, possibly they were on ice-cream nights…as well as on days when they discussed their worst moments.

'Rosa had a specialist doctor appointment in Milan—that's why she was with them. She wasn't coming to lunch…'

There was an edge to his voice when he spoke about

Rosa, but Susie said nothing, just listened when he gave his sad conclusion.

'They crashed just after take-off.'

'How did you find out?' she asked, imagining him waiting in a restaurant. 'Did you guess something was wrong when they didn't show?'

'No, I got a call from Christos. He said I had to get back here. They didn't know how bad it was, but I think he knew...'

His hand felt like ice—so much so that she wanted to hold it tighter, to warm it, but she dared not move, scared that he'd pull his hand back or stop talking.

'We all came here, waiting for news. Gio's reaction was dreadful. He collapsed, and seemed to know straight away there was no chance they'd survived. Sev was in the Middle East... The guy had to fly back not knowing if anyone had. I told him there was still hope...' He gave a wry smile. 'I'd seen the wreckage, the fire, but I really thought there might be a chance they'd got out. They hadn't, of course.'

'How do you...?' She swallowed. 'Sorry, stupid question.'

'How do you cope with something like that?' He asked the stupid question for her. 'Gio took to his bed—perhaps for a year. Sev went back to work a week after the funerals. I don't think he's stopped working since.'

'And you?'

'I was practical—calling people, sorting the funerals, seeing the lawyers, going through the wills...' He gave a dark smile. 'That said, I was up before dawn every day, scouring the accident site.'

'Looking for what?'

'Something.' He took a breath. 'Anything.'

'Did you find anything?'

'Not really. In the end I hired a specialist company—they had tools to comb the hillside. They salvaged a couple of small things.' He raised his eyebrows, as if surprised that he'd said that. 'I've never told Gio or Sev that anything was found.'

'Can I ask why not?'

He shook his head and it was left at that.

The gorgeous, lazy afternoon had turned sombre, at least for Susie. Dante, though, was talking normally to Christos as she put on her coat. Then she realised that this must be his normal—that he lived daily with all the sadness she'd felt hearing his story. No wonder he couldn't bear to come home...

'For you,' Christos said, handing her a beautiful basket of all the wines and cheeses she'd especially liked, and some truffled honey too.

'How gorgeous!'

'Susie's bringing her parents here in a few weeks,' Dante said as they left—only Susie wasn't so sure now, wondering how it might feel to be here without Dante.

It was a forty-minute drive back through the hillsides, and Dante looked out of the window this time—at the De Santis winery as they passed, and the church where Sev and Rosa had married...where Rosa now lay.

She heard the whir of a window closing and saw the divider between them and the driver was now shut. Dante's hand came to her hair. She turned fully around and was met by desire.

She guessed this was Dante's preferred method of escape.

It was her preferred method now, too.

Because all the horrors that had been discussed seemed to fade, his tongue chasing them away, his kiss raw with passion, his hands tight around her waist.

There was no more talking, because it hurt too much, and it was so nice to be kissed in the back of a car, to feel his hands slip between her thighs.

'Those tights are an issue,' he told her, his hand creeping up her inner thigh.

'Dante...' She looked towards the closed partition.

'We're just kissing,' he told her.

But she knew he lied—because even if that was all their shadows appeared to be doing, she could feel his hand moving further up her thigh, then the firm massage of his palm through her tights...

She wished they were gone too. But they remained. And he cupped her warmth and stroked her, and then he left her mouth. His head was heavy against her as he kissed her neck and the stroking of his fingers did not stop.

'Come on...' he urged her—as if it was necessary...as if her pleasure was completely required.

His mouth was high on her shoulder—or was it the base of her neck? But it was wet, and thorough, and she felt a low spread of warmth. His mouth returned to her lips, as if he knew before she did what was happening, and then his lips were over hers, but not moving, swallowing her gasps as her bottom lifted a touch and her thighs closed tight around his hand.

'Nice...'

She wanted to close her eyes, to rest her head back, to catch her breath. So she did.

And it was Dante who pulled down the hem of her dress, so they were only holding hands as the car swept into his driveway, and Susie had never felt happier, or bolder, or more desperate to get inside.

'Grazie,' Dante said as the car door opened.

She forgot the basket of goodies, but he remembered and carried it up the steps, then opened up the door.

They stepped into his home and she shrugged off her coat. She caught the smoky scent of fire, and wondered if it was from her, but then she glanced into the lounge.

'Someone's been in.'

'The housekeeper.' Dante clearly did not want diversions.

'Is she in here?' Susie asked, walking into the room.

'Of course not,' he told her.

And Susie was about to turn, more than ready to be taken straight to bed, but then his hands came down to her waist and slid up to her breasts. She felt the press of him behind her and relished the roam of his hands and how he wasn't shamed by his desire.

He turned her, and she wanted to be stripped, wanted her clothes to disappear. She knew he felt the same because his jumper was off, so she kissed his chest, the flat nipples, and she wanted to sink lower, but fought the desire as she'd never done that before.

And yet her hands slipped down as they got back to kissing and she felt him through fabric, felt how he hardened beneath her palm, and her fingers ached for more contact.

She attempted to undo his belt as they kissed, but thankfully he dealt with that, and then she was holding him, stroking him, feeling the velvet skin on her palm. She looked down and was fascinated, and the desire to sink down and taste him refused to relent.

Her mouth moved as if of its own accord and she followed the trail her lips made, closing her eyes as they bypassed his chest. Her mouth strayed lower and kissed his stomach, tasted his salty skin.

He was too tall for comfort, and for a moment she kissed his thighs. And perhaps he saw her struggle, because he guided her so she sat on a couch. Susie had no idea of its colour. Apart from the gorgeous fire, she hadn't really taken in her surroundings. It was ridiculously comfortable, though, and the cushions soft on her bottom. She relished her unhurried exploration, holding him and dropping little kisses along his length, and then suddenly she became aware she was fully dressed.

'Should I take off my clothes?' she asked, and looked up to see his frown. 'I've never done this.'

'Do you want to?'

'Oh, yes.'

'Why do you think you have to get undressed?'

'To turn you on?'

'That's not an issue,' Dante said, and his hand closed over her own.

Together they stroked his thick length, and then back to her came the deep pull of desire, and there was no reason to resist it.

'I love that you've never done this,' he said in a gravelly voice.

But perhaps her tentative mouth knew what to do, because when she took him in, he made a breathless sound that she knew from when they were in bed.

She tasted him, and his hands guided her as she took her time, taking him in, then a little deeper...

Dante had more control than most.

Not to impress his lovers—more because he held back, even in bed.

Sex was usually necessary and frequent.

In contrast, this was ponderous and tender.

There was an internal fight building in him. At first he thought it was frustration, at her untutored mouth taking him too gently, or her hand gripping too lightly. But then he realised the fight was with himself. The temptation he was fighting wasn't to place his hand over hers and show her how to move more roughly, nor to move her head lower and tell her she would not hurt him.

No, it was none of that.

He was fighting not to stroke her hair, not to smooth it back so he could see her, not to touch her cheek.

And so he told her how good she felt, how good he felt.

But he held back on telling her of the light and the joy she had brought to him.

'*Non ti fermare!*' he told her. 'I want to see you,' he added, smoothing her hair back, seeing the reddened cheeks that had been so pale before.

She was lost. But she was no longer shy or unsure, just loving the taste of him, and the feel of his hands smoothing back her hair, over and over, then cupping her cheeks tenderly.

And his thrusts didn't daunt her. She was hot between her legs, her breasts heavy beneath her dress. She was aching below and deeply turned on.

There was a slight flurry of panic as she felt him swell, and rush, and then it was the sexiest moment... Because she heard him shout, as if his own climax had caught him unawares, and she tasted him, on the edge of her own orgasm as she lifted her head.

His eyes were closed, but he pulled her up to join him, both standing breathless, their only regret that there was no bed to sink into.

'Come on,' he said.

His bed was made and it was bliss to be stripped before she got into it. He even took her boots off.

'What's this?' he asked of her silver underwear.

'I bought it today.'

They lay together and she adored just lying there, talking, half asleep and yet awake.

'You were in a relationship for...?' he asked.

'Two years.'

'And yet...' He let out a reluctant laugh. 'I don't want to think about it, but...' he was clearly curious '...you've never...?'

'No.' She shook her head. 'I told you: we were very boring in that way.'

'That's not boring. That's...' He thought for a moment. 'Sad.'

'Yes,' she agreed. 'I tried to liven things up, but...' She sighed. 'I don't think he was that interested in me.'

'Yet you stayed?'

'No, I ended things...' She looked up. 'He's the only person I've slept with.'

'Okay...' He was obviously thinking. 'So, what drew you to a man with no passion?'

'It wasn't that bad,' she said, and laughed. But it soon changed. 'It wasn't that good. I just didn't know it. We're good, aren't we?' she said.

'Yes.'

His hand stroked her arm and her hair, and then moved back to her arm. 'I'm going to return the favour,' he told her.

'Please, no...' She cringed at the very thought. 'I could never...'

Then she paused, because until a short while ago she'd never thought she could want to take someone in her mouth. She thought for a moment, but then shook her head.

'No,' she said. 'I don't think I'd like that.'

What she really liked was this: lying half awake, half asleep...sharing confidences...as if some kind of truth serum had been slipped into them while they slept.

CHAPTER SIX

'How is it Monday already?' Dante asked.

'You've got to go to the jewellers.'

'Don't remind me.'

'It will be nice.'

He didn't answer that.

'You've got class this morning?' he asked.

'I do,' she said. 'Then a lunchtime shift.'

She stared into the thin morning light, loving being wrapped in his arms, and asked the question she was dreading the answer to.

'What time do you fly?'

'I haven't booked it yet.' He yawned, and was silent for a moment. Then, 'Perhaps I could fly back early tomorrow morning.'

Susie swallowed, her delight at the prospect of another night tempered with a lick of uncertainty. It was all very well for him, with his million and one exes—he was clearly used to goodbyes.

She thought back to her one attempt yesterday. That had been hard enough. Now, it felt near-impossible to say goodbye without crying. Oh, she wanted to be sophisticated, and to kiss him and walk away. But, while she'd accepted this was temporary, her emotions were joining their little sex party.

'I thought you only did one night?' She tried to speak as if it were to tease or joke. 'We're already on two.'

'I thought I only had one night when I said that,' Dante pointed out.

She thought back to him asking her to dinner—that was before Gio had decided to go to the jewellers. 'So, you do have longer relationships?'

'I wouldn't call them "relationships", but, yes of course. Short-lived, but not just one night.'

'Do you ever get involved? Too involved?'

'No,' Dante said. 'Now, I should shower and get ready, or Gio will be waiting for me in his hat and coat.'

Dante was lying. The truth was he didn't get involved, and always left at the first sign... And if he said that to Susie... Well, it would mean he'd been the same with her as with others.

Never.

This weekend had been a complete exception and he knew he should end things.

What the hell was he doing, suggesting another night?

Yet, he wanted another night.

He came out of the shower and Susie was lying there, gazing at the ceiling. And then she looked over to him.

'Can I ask something?'

'You can.'

'When you end things...'

'It's not just me that ends things. I always make it clear that I don't want to get too close, and...' He paused, took a shirt from the wardrobe, and then answered the question. 'If it *is* me ending things, I just say it's over.'

'And?'

'My assistant sends flowers...a gift.'

'A little bauble?'

'I don't gift jewellery,' Dante said. 'Antonia generally chooses.' He buttoned up his shirt.

'Does Antonia write the card?'

'I think the florist does,' he responded. 'I'll make coffee.'

'I like milk,' Susie said. 'I'll get my own coffee on the way.'

She didn't want a card from his assistant, or flowers, or a gift.

As she showered and dressed she tried to pull herself out of a slight panic. She was torn between wanting another night and the farewell that was surely to come.

They left together, but as Dante walked down the steps Susie stopped, in the middle of wrapping her scarf, and saw all she'd missed last night.

'Oh!' She was taken aback by the view...the sheer beauty of where they were. Behind the elegant houses she could see the Tuscan hills. 'You can see the hills!' She spun around, and whichever way she looked the views were to die for. 'And the walls.' Everywhere she looked it was like a postcard. 'It's so gorgeous... How did I miss this?'

'We were a bit distracted.'

'True.' Susie laughed and, refusing to be rushed, stood and gazed down the almost deserted avenue.

Dante, who'd seemed impatient to get on, followed her gaze. 'It is stunning,' he agreed. 'In spring, the magnolia trees flower.'

'They're all magnolia trees?' She stood, trying to picture it in bloom. 'They're my favourite flowers.'

'Come the spring, you're in for a treat.'

'No...' She shook her head, hit by a sudden wave of pensiveness. It was possibly not fitting, over flowers she would never see, yet it briefly knocked her off kilter, and she could feel her smile slipping away, her shoulders drooping. 'I'll be in Florence by then,' she said.

Her voice sounded hollow, when usually she spoke of Florence with excitement, but it dawned on her that possibly it wouldn't be a floral display she'd be pining for.

Oh, God!

She looked down the street and then back to Dante. The collar was up on his coat, and he looked brooding and completely irresistible, and for the first time she glimpsed the hell of getting over him.

Did it really have to end?

Were there never exceptions to his temporary lover rule?

Any chance for an extension?

She'd been so happy with one night. Deliriously happy with two. And now...?

'Susie? Everything okay?' he checked.

Why not tell him what she was thinking? Susie pondered. For it was as if last night had somehow freed her—as if the liberty he'd brought to her body had also converted her mind. She would tell him how she felt. And maybe...just possibly...

'I was just...' she began.

But it was as if some sleeping guardian angel had been startled awake and had grabbed her by the collar of her trench coat, squeezing her throat tight on the surely forbidden words.

Do not fall for him, Susie, the angel warned.

You might be a bit late, she replied silently, though thankfully the moment of madness was over.

She liked the honesty between them, how he'd told her to speak up and say how she felt, but in this instance she knew that honesty possibly wasn't the best policy when dealing with a playboy of Dante's calibre.

So she pushed back her shoulders, conjured a smile and dashed down the steps to his side.

'I just adore magnolias.'

Sure enough, Gio was dressed and ready.

'You're late,' he told Dante.

'No...' Dante glanced at the clock and saw he was actually on time.

He didn't point it out to Gio, though. He knew this was very emotional for him.

They were silent as they passed the church where Dante knew his grandparents had married, then they turned and walked along a small cobbled street. Naturally Gio knew practically everyone they passed, and stopped for a greeting, but as they approached the small group of shops he paused.

'I want to ensure all the jewels are taken care of,' he said. 'And then I might have a private conversation with Signor Adino.'

'Of course,' Dante said.

'It might take some time.'

'No problem.'

The jewellers had been there long before Dante was born, with its dark wooden façade and gorgeous windows that displayed both modern and antique jewels.

'You and Sev used to look at the watches here.'

'We did.'

He'd forgotten that. They had been there often. Not just with Gio. Mamma would sit trying on rings, and all the other things that had seemed boring, and he and Sev had stared at the clocks and watches.

He saw the flash of his own stainless-steel watch now, as he rang the bell for their private appointment. The store would be closed to others.

'Welcome, Signor Casadio,' said Signor Adino as he opened the heavy glass door. 'Ah, and Sev...'

The jeweller stopped and laughed at his mistake, and Dante felt the sweep of Signor Adino's eyes briefly register his scar.

'I knew it was you who made the appointment, Dante, but for a moment I thought you were Sev. It's been such a long time.'

Such a long time.

He'd excluded himself as much as possible from life here for more than a decade.

Signor Adino locked the door behind them as Gio walked over to the rear counter and placed down the black jewellery pouch that contained so much of his life. His shaking hands opened it up—he clearly wanted to do this himself.

'There is a stone loose on this choker,' Gio said, and his voice was trembling as the jeweller put on his magnifying glasses. 'I remember you making this for her...' Gio took out a handkerchief, then turned to Dante. 'He's a good salesman. I had to purchase a silver hand mirror—'

'So Signora Casadio could see it when she put it on!' Signor Adino carried on.

Only Dante wasn't listening. He was staring at the spread of jewels on the black velvet—some dulled, but still attempting to shine, some that had belonged to his mother. There was even the cross and chain his father had worn when they were small.

It was the pieces that were missing that punished him the most.

Lost in the accident on the hills.

He thought of the two stones sitting in his safe back in Milan. He would really prefer to leave Gio to it, and yet he stood beside him, watching as each piece was laid out and one by one the jeweller made notes in a handwritten ledger.

Who the hell still used carbon paper?

Finally, the list was complete and the copy handed to Gio, who watched as the jewels and so many of his memories were carefully taken out to the back of the shop to be lovingly tended to.

'Are you okay?' Gio checked with Dante, when surely it should be the other way around.

'Of course.'

And with the past taken care of, the jeweller returned and smiled to Gio. 'I have everything set up for you, Signor Casadio.'

'I might be a while,' Gio said.

Dante nodded, watching as Gio moved behind the counter, no doubt to choose the stone for Mimi's ring.

He wandered around the small store, looking at the watches. There was a beautiful old gold one...

He glanced down at his own luxury watch and told himself he did not need another one. Anyway, he didn't wear gold.

And then from nowhere a memory assailed him, of standing on this very spot, with Sev beside him, not with his mother looking at rings, but with his father at the counter. Collecting a ring.

Turning to Sev, he had asked a question. 'What's an eternity ring?'

Slamming closed that memory, he walked away from the watches and crossed the floor of the tiny jewellers in two strides. For a while he stood unseeing, staring at the lavish displays, wishing to God they weren't locked in.

Then a burst of laughter from the office hauled him back to the present, and he looked with mild interest at some of the more modern pieces.

His attention was held by one. A necklace of sunflowers—a beautiful swirl of gemstones and precious metals—and beneath it a sticker that proclaimed it sold. His eyes moved to rubies arranged like a field of wild poppies and set in white gold. They weren't slender chains...more like subtle jewelled garlands with leaves.

He pulled his head back when he realised the jeweller had come out of the office and was standing behind him.

'Signor Casadio wanted a few moments alone.'

'Grazie.' Dante nodded, grateful for the time taken and the kindness shown to his grandfather—and he knew it wasn't just because the Casadios had once been regular clients, it was how things were done here. 'Are these your work?' he asked.

'They are.' Signor Adino nodded.

'Exquisite.'

'Thank you. They are a labour of love.'

Perhaps he could break another rule? He wasn't one for gifts, or romantic gestures, and certainly gave nothing as personal as jewellery. But he and Susie had got personal, and even if it could never last this weekend had meant a lot.

He'd heard the edge in her voice as she'd asked about the gifts he gave, about how he would end things.

Nicely.

Nicer than he'd ever been, perhaps?

'Do you have magnolias?'

'I don't.'

'Anything similar?'

'No...' The jeweller shook his head. 'These two are bespoke pieces—they are being collected this week. They are certainly not impulse purchases,' he scolded lightly. 'They take weeks to make. First a design is decided on, then the mould is cast...'

'So, not for me then?' Dante got the message and gave a wry laugh. 'I was just...' He didn't know quite what he'd been thinking, but then he smiled and looked up as Gio came out. 'Okay?'

'Yes.' Gio nodded and came over to thank Signor Adino profusely.

'So,' Dante said as they walked back to Gio's. 'What did you choose?'

'That is for Mimi to reveal,' Gio retorted. 'I haven't even asked her to marry me yet. Haven't I taught you anything?'

Dante saw him back to his house, and then his grandfather said he was going for a sleep.

'You no doubt have a flight to catch,' Gio said as he farewelled him. 'Thank you for taking the day off today.'

'Any time,' Dante said. 'Well, not any time,' he warned as he kissed Gio goodbye. 'No getting married too soon; I have a case coming up...'

'I know you do.'

Gio certainly looked happier than when he'd arrived, Dante thought as he walked along the walls in the direction of home.

At times he had felt happy too.

But he knew he couldn't stay in bed with Susie for ever.

He sat on a bench and thought of how their conversations had started to deepen.

He'd wanted to know more about her.

And yet...

It was still hell to be here.

He thought of all those jewels splayed out on the velvet, and his grandfather thinking him cold because he could barely bring himself to look at them.

Susie was right. Old memories tainted the future.

Perhaps he would suggest she come to Milan this weekend?

He thought of her busy schedule, and the scant direct flights.

Then he closed his eyes in despair as he realised Gio had been right to doubt he was over the accident.

Dante got on and off helicopters with little thought. He just accepted that he had to, and took the risk...

But he could not stand the thought of Susie up in one.

'Susie?' The language teacher smiled. 'You are distracted today.'

'Sorry...'

Susie apologised, and tried to focus on the class, but her mind was in a hundred different places, and when it was time for a break, rather than find coffee and a chat she slipped off in search of peace.

The school had a magnificent balcony and Susie stepped out—just for some air and a moment.

Gosh, she was going to start crying, she thought, trying to remind herself that a few days ago she hadn't known him. The last time she'd attended class Dante hadn't even factored into her life. Perhaps it was better that she fired off a message now and told him she couldn't make it tonight.

Or maybe she'd decide after her lunchtime shift?

Then she stilled, for there on a bench he sat, staring out to the hills. She pulled back from the edge of the balcony and tried to tell herself to just go back to class.

Then she watched as he tipped his head back, as she might at the hairdresser's. But that only described the motion he made—it didn't explain why that movement had tears spilling down her cheeks.

She was witnessing agony.

'How was class?' Dante asked, letting the exhausted Susie in.

'It was okay,' she said.

'Work?'

'Long,' she admitted, taking off her awful shoes.

He helped her with her scarf and coat.

He sounded normal, and he certainly looked beautiful—no sign of the man she'd seen sitting alone and despairing on that bench.

'How was the jeweller's?' she asked.

'It was okay,' he told her. 'I'm not allowed to know what he chose for Mimi, of course. I meant to call Maria…'

'Who's Maria?'

'My housekeeper. I forgot to tell her I would be here tonight. I was going to ask her to get some food in. But I'll call for something—or we can go out?'

'Or I could make something?' Susie said.

'You've been at work.'

'I work most days,' Susie said, and smiled. 'And I eat most days too.'

She liked how he laughed and kissed her, and it was heaven to be back here. Really, she'd been stupid to think she couldn't handle it. It was just one more night, and she wanted to be here, so...

'Anyway...' She wriggled from his arms. 'I've been dying to get into your kitchen.' She laughed at his expression. 'Don't worry, Dante, I just miss cooking. There are only two little gas rings at the apartment, and a microwave and a toaster.'

'I really don't have any food.'

She opened up his cupboards and then peered into his fridge. 'And you had the cheek to tell me off about your grandfather's meagre fridge contents!' She saw a lonely tub of ricotta and a couple of other cheeses. 'I'll be fine with these.'

'You're sure?'

She nodded. 'There's a recipe I've been dying to try,' she told him, taking down a bag of walnuts from a cupboard. 'You've got most things I need.'

'Do you want some wine?'

'No, thank you.' She pulled out some flour and looked at his glass. 'I thought you didn't like wine?'

'Hmm...' He put down his glass and rather elegantly hopped onto the large marble bench, watching her pulling out jars he clearly hadn't known he had. 'I'm seriously hungry,' he warned, obviously not believing that nuts, cheese and some flour could be turned into much.

'I know.'

'Hey, Susie? What if your cooking is terrible?' he asked, making her smile. 'Do I have to pretend I like it?' he teased.

'Since when did you ever do that?' She smirked. 'You can give me your usual honest opinion.'

She was loving this…making pasta, stretching it, running it through the machine and watching as the lovely soft white sheets came out.

Dante sat watching her. It was unusual to see anyone other than Maria in his kitchen—and certainly he didn't sit and watch his housekeeper cook.

'I've got to go to court,' he told her. 'The wife read the husband's letter yesterday.'

'But he only posted it on Friday.'

'Through her door. Where he shouldn't even have been.'

'Gosh…'

'And he's not supposed to contact her, so another rap on the knuckles for me. He's offered, in his own handwriting, far more than had been agreed. Now he wants to change his mind. What a mess…'

'Do you like the wine?' she asked.

'I do…' He took another sip of wine, unable to voice more, because he could hardly believe he was drinking wine and thinking about the winery.

Thinking about taking on a little more responsibility for it.

He was grateful for the loud buzz as she blended walnuts, yet the large kitchen still felt peaceful.

Gio had never legally passed the business on to Dante's father, even though it had caused a few arguments…

'You'll get it when I'm gone,' Gio would declare. *'For now, it stays with me.'*

And that had proved important when tragedy had struck…

'My father had very big ideas for the winery,' he told her. 'Though Gio wouldn't let him get his hands on it. Rosa's family did too. They wanted to blend the two of them…'

Susie looked up.

'But Gio was having none of it. He would say, "You can do what you want with it when I'm gone…"'

'Did you ever want to be a part of it?'

'No—nor did Sev. Maybe we would have got involved somewhere down the line, but we wanted our own careers first.'

He watched as she placed little balls of mixture on the sheet of pasta, and found that watching Susie made it all too easy to voice his thoughts out loud. To *want* to voice them.

'If my father had been a shareholder on his death that share would have passed to Sev and I. And any of our spouses would have had a stake.'

'Ah, but you're going to be single for ever,' Susie said.

There were little parcels of ravioli all over his bench now, and she was concentrating on her sauce.

'Sev wasn't single.'

'No,' Susie agreed, and turned to him and offered a sympathetic smile. 'Rosa died, though.'

'Where there's a will there's a family…' Dante said. 'Do they say that in England?'

'I don't know.'

Susie gave a small laugh and got on with tasting her sauce.

Dante knew she didn't get it that if Gio had not been so wise then Rosa's family might have had a claim. It was the sort of thing that had kept him in the library for hours, long before her death, reading all the details in the books that lined the walls.

While he'd never anticipated losing his family, Dante had always been sure the De Santises had been trying to get hold of Gio's rich, fertile land and become a part of the successful winery business.

He took a sip of his wine—blackcurrant with a hint of pepper…

If the De Santises had had their way they'd be drinking vinegar by now.

Yes, Gio had been wise.

And, yes, perhaps he should have spoken to him—at least about the legal side...

Not about the sex or the pregnancy that never was.

That would be too much for Gio.

Too much for anyone.

'Nearly there,' Susie said, walking past the bench as she went to get a large copper saucepan.

He trapped her with his legs as she passed. 'It looks great.'

'You haven't tasted it yet.'

'Can I help?' he asked, knowing it was almost done.

'You can lay the table.'

'Or...' He pulled her in, looked at the flour on her cheeks and on her black dress, and found he was more than happy not to think about the De Santis family any more. 'We could eat in bed...'

'I want it to be nice.' She looked at him. 'I haven't cooked in for ever.'

'I shall lay the table, then.'

He did indeed lay the table—the grand table in his dining room—and he even lit candles.

'Susie!' he called as she passed by with plates. 'In here.'

She stepped in and her jaw dropped—not so much at the stunning polished table and the jade walls, but at the silver candelabra.

'I meant the coffee table... And candles?' she commented as she put down their plates. 'That's very romantic of you, Signor Casadio.'

'I think the food calls for it,' he said, turning out the main lights.

'We'll see...'

'Take a seat,' Dante said, and held out her chair.

'Thank you.'

Susie felt nervous as he sat down and looked at what she'd

made. She always did when she tried something new, but
somehow tonight it mattered more than ever.

'Ricotta ravioli with a walnut sauce…'

Dante looked at the food before him. He had eaten in many,
many fine restaurants and this wouldn't be out of place in
any of them—and all made from the scant selection in his
cupboards.

He looked at the little garnish of parsley. 'It looks very
nice,' he said, then turned his plate and nodded.

He picked up a fork and sliced a piece of ravioli, then took
a mouthful and tasted it as carefully as Gio would taste wine.

Susie almost wished he'd just dive in and declare it 'nice' or
'awful', as her ex had. But then she'd hated it when he did that.

Dante took his time.

'Okay…' he said at last, when he'd swallowed the first
mouthful. And she knew he wasn't saying that about her food.

He thought for a moment, and took another taste of her
walnut sauce, before delivering his conclusion.

'Tell Cucou that you want a trial.' He looked right at her.
'Demand it.'

'I can't demand it!' She laughed away the very thought.
'Is it nice, though?'

'Susie, I was always going to be polite, no matter if it was
nice or not. I was always going to say it was delicious, because I am polite and you cooked it. But this belongs in any
top restaurant I have eaten in. I want to eat it all immediately.
Even if you offered sex, right now on the table, I would want
to finish my food first.'

'Honestly?'

'Offer me sex on the table and I'll prove it.'

She laughed, and yet she felt close to crying. It was the

first time someone had really, properly talked with her about her cooking.

'Tell them you want a trial,' he repeated.

'I already have. They're not interested. I don't have experience... I can't speak the language.'

'Tell them food *is* your language, and then suggest they give you a chance or you'll walk out.'

'I need the job.'

'Susie, they're testing you. You have to be tough to survive in a kitchen like that. They would not have you preparing food for my grandfather if they didn't think the world of you. He is a very well thought of man here.'

'Yes...'

'Stand up for yourself. You might find they are just waiting for you to do so.'

She'd never considered such a thing.

It was a gorgeous night.

'I don't know what was better,' Dante said a whole lot later, as they lay there breathless and sated. 'The food or the sex...'

Such a gorgeous night...

So much so she forgot to dread the morning.

Even as it arrived...

CHAPTER SEVEN

'I LIKE THIS…' Susie admitted.

'What?'

'Lying in bed talking…'

They hadn't really slept, and now morning was creeping in. No beams of light, but she could see their hands knotted together on his stomach as she lay with her head on his chest. And as brilliant, as dazzling and as whirlwind as the weekend had been, and as fabulous as the sex was, it was these quiet moments, just talking, that she'd cherish deeply. It was where they were closest to one another, and the truth serum seemed to reach its peak dose around dawn…

'I hear Juliet and Louanna chatting most mornings,' she told him.

'Are they partners?'

'No!' She thumped his chest lightly. 'They get up before me, that's all. I hear them discussing their music, and people I don't know. It just reminds me…'

'Of what?'

'Growing up, I had my own room,' Susie explained. 'While my sisters got to share.'

'*Got* to share?' he checked. 'Wouldn't you want your own room?'

She laughed. 'We don't all live in mansions. It was a three-bedroom home. Usually the eldest gets their own room, but the twins wanted to be together,' she explained. 'All my friends said I was lucky.'

'But you didn't feel so lucky?'

'It sounded as if they were having a party every night. And then came discussions about boys and make-up and...'

'What about birthdays?' Dante said.

'What about them?'

'I think Gio said you were close in age to the twins?'

'They're just over a year older.' She took a breath. 'So our parties were all lumped together. It was a case of two against one,' she said. 'I always wanted to have a fairy party or dress up...'

'What did your sisters want?'

'To go to the cinema, or the zoo, or...' She thought back. 'I remember this man with reptiles came to the garden.' She shuddered. 'I was very young.'

He laughed. 'What's your first memory?'

'I can't remember.'

'Come on...'

'I was in my pushchair...' Clearly, he wasn't up on the names of baby paraphernalia. 'A stroller? And I saw a lady smiling and saying nice things about me to my mother. Then the twins came out of the shop with my father and she just started admiring them...' She gave a muted laugh. 'I threw my dummy out.' He frowned. 'Pacifier?'

'Ah...' He smiled. 'For attention?'

'I threw it again and again. See? I'm not nice.'

'Are you jealous?' he asked.

She was about to defend herself—to answer as she had before and say of course she was not—but she felt hot tears splashing out, along with the truth.

'So very jealous.' She left his arms and sat up, almost leapt out of bed, as if startled by her own truth. 'So damn jealous... The twins, the twins, the twins...' she parroted.

And out burst almost twenty-five years' worth of stored bitter tears.

'Hey...'

Emotional outbursts did not move him, but feeling her crumple, seeing the wet tears, hearing the choking voice, he was both horrified and stunned that their light, playful conversation had turned so dark.

Dante had been provoking her for the truth, but the depth of her pain stunned him. And yet he was oddly pleased to hold the real Susie, to feel this hot ball of emotion in his arms.

'You can be jealous,' he told her. 'Why not?'

'It's wrong, though. I love them, but...' She was really crying now. 'There was a school play...'

She told him how stunning they'd been as angels...and how heads always turned whenever they passed. And about the shared bedroom again. Out it all came.

'They even got beautiful names—Cassandra and Celia, I got Susan.' She halted, as if stunned by her own vitriol. 'Oh, God, I sound so...'

'Jealous,' he said. 'And no wonder.' He was practical. 'Next time your mother accuses you, say, *Yes, I am jealous, so perhaps you could be more thoughtful.*'

'I doubt that would work.' She closed her eyes and took a breath and he pulled her back down. 'Do you get jealous?' she asked.

He thought for a moment. 'No.'

'What's *your* first memory?'

'I think getting a smack.' He laughed. 'I wandered off on the beach.' He thought of his mother. 'My mother was furious.'

'Scared?'

'Yes. That was the only time I saw her angry. When I was in

the jewellers yesterday—' He stopped. He really hadn't meant to go there. But then he looked at her wet lashes and reasoned that she'd told him some painful stuff. 'I remembered being there when my mother chose some stones for a ring. She was laughing. Then a few weeks later we went with my father to pick the ring up. I asked Sev what an eternity ring was.'

'What did he say?'

'I can't recall,' Dante admitted. 'You remember I told you that I had people comb the accident site? They found two rubies from that ring.'

'And you haven't told anyone?'

'No, it would be too much for Gio. He cried over a loose stone on Nonna's choker...'

She frowned, clearly still not getting it.

'I don't know if my mother took her ring off, and that was how the stones didn't shatter in the fire,' he said. 'Or...'

She was still frowning, so he was more direct.

'There was nothing of them left intact.'

'Oh, God,' she said, which was entirely the wrong thing, but he found he didn't mind.

'It's fine. Gio doesn't need to know. They're in an envelope in a safe. I don't look at them or know what to do with them. I spend most of my life with people who are fighting over things and I don't get it. I can't imagine fighting over a house, or a yacht, or anything.'

'Why haven't you told Sev?'

Dante shook his head, and although it was clear he was telling her to leave it, Susie saw he was looking right into her eyes.

It was the first time in her life she'd truly felt close to another person—as if it was in this room, in this conversation, that she completely belonged.

Susie stared into his dark eyes and told herself that was ridiculous.

She had family, friends, work… And, yes, she was loved.

But in this moment, she was in the right place, and nothing and no one could invade it.

His hand brushed back the hair on her forehead, and they were still staring at the other.

'Suuu-zeee…' he said, changing the topic in the nicest of ways. 'I think it's a beautiful name.'

'Only when *you* say it.'

He gave a very gentle smile as they continued to stare right into each other's eyes.

'Maybe…' he said, and moved to kiss her.

She saw his eyes draw nearer, felt the warmth of his skin even before their lips had met, and she knew she was about to be kissed.

It was thrilling, even though she'd been kissed by Dante many times. This kiss was soft, as were his hands, and feeling his mouth on hers caused an involuntary sob…

She revelled in his citrussy cologne and the warm caress of his tongue, in how he stroked the side of her aching breast as her arms coiled around his neck. His head moved down and he took her breast in his mouth. She heard herself moan again, felt the slide of his hands on her hips, the tempo moving to a mutual urgency.

He pulled the pillows from the bed and she lay beneath him. And even though he moved to his elbows it was the lower weight of him that had her breathless. His hungry kiss made her feel as if she were being crushed by desire.

'Dante…'

His mouth was at her ear, kissing the shell, and there were myriad sensations. His thigh was between her legs, and she was already parting them, and his groan as he squeezed inside her spoke for them both.

She arched up and pressed her hands into him, her body begging for urgent relief, but his thrusts were slow and measured.

'Slow down,' he told her, denying her haste.

'I can't.'

She spoke not just for her body, but for every part of her. She did not know how to slow things down now he'd appeared in her life. She was aching with desire, tearful at the prospect of missing him, and reckless with her heart. All Susie knew was that she wanted more than she'd had. It was as if everything was in tune—as if loneliness had been banished and she could not hold back.

And suddenly she felt a rush of fury that he was holding back, taking her slowly. So she arched again, impatiently. 'Please...'

And at her urging Susie found out just how much he'd been holding back.

He took her with an intensity she hadn't realised until now that she craved.

'Suuu-zeee...' he said, as perfectly as he had that first night, calling her name as only he could. Filling her, consuming her, and making her temporarily his.

And she didn't want it to be over, didn't want their time to end. Her eyes flicked open, only to be met by his.

A single look that evoked a thousand questions.

'How?' she asked as he took her.

For a second she thought he might answer her nonsensical question, but instead Dante closed his eyes, and went back into his head.

'How...' she demanded and if she had nails, they would have dug in his back, but instead she clung on. She kissed his salty shoulder and wanted to bite. Again fury rushed through her—for how could he want her in this moment, then say goodbye the next.

And it was goodbye, for he was releasing into her.

How could they be over, she wanted to beg, but there were no words left. Feeling him come, hearing his passionate shout had her fury twisting into desire, delivering an orgasm so deep it took all thought away.

When her eyes opened she saw his were closed as she dragged breath back into her lungs.

'How?' Susie asked again, as intimate pulses faded.

Of course he didn't answer.

Dante rarely allowed emotion in the bedroom.

Pleasure, yes.

But his heart had been sealed so long ago he'd forgotten it existed.

Yet it had emerged in recent days and now it thumped in his chest.

He took in a deep breath, knowing there was no way ahead for them.

He'd heard her question.

How did they do this?

Certainly he didn't want her to be endlessly here waiting for occasional visits, but nor did he want her whirring her way through the air to Milan.

For what?

They were too close for comfort. What had felt right a moment ago now felt unfamiliar and unwelcome, and he knew he was too dark for her light.

He could hear her talking, apologising for her feelings. Oh, she didn't allude to the question begged in the throes of lovemaking instead admitting to being embarrassed by her earlier tears and what she'd revealed about being jealous.

'So there you have it,' Susie said. 'The fatal flaw...my Achilles' heel.'

'It's really not that bad,' Dante said.

And then, as she often did, Susie practised her Italian.

'Qual è l'azione peggiore che hai impegnato?'

Dante frowned as he deciphered her dreadful pronunciation. 'What is the worst action I have ever committed?'

He started to smile—he knew she'd got the words wrong, and had been trying to get him to share—but then his smile faded.

He reached down to rescue one of the pillows that had been scattered by their lovemaking, but then he put his hand behind his head and lay flat.

He was tired of carrying his secret.

Possibly he knew his truth would deal with things and push her away for ever.

How?

Dante knew how to end them—'I slept with my brother's wife.'

Susie looked over at him. Watched as Dante stared at the ceiling…

'Is that why…?'

She didn't finish the question. Of course that would have caused the brothers to fall out.

But then Dante gave a small shake of his head. 'Sev doesn't know.'

For a second she wanted to sit up, to hug her knees, to resist looking at him—for surely there were few betrayals worse than that? But she was held by the agony in his eyes, and she knew that whatever her own feelings were on the subject he surely didn't need to hear them.

She didn't doubt Dante was already burning in his own guilty hell.

She had never been entrusted with something so big, and she touched his arm, not knowing what to say, but trying. 'Was it…?' She tried to keep the shaky note from her voice. 'Did it go on for long?'

'It was once.'

He closed his eyes and took a deep breath, and Susie thought he was trying to banish the memory rather than summon it.

'I was in Milan, a student. I'd just passed my first-year exams.'

She frowned, trying to get her head around things. Surely Dante had been at the end of his studies when Sev had got married? She stayed silent rather than speak.

'Even back then I never got involved with anyone who came from here. But she was in Milan for a visit and we met up.' His laugh was both dark and resigned. 'We were nineteen—you know what it's like...'

Susie had had no idea what *anything* was like at nineteen—at least not on the dating front. She'd been awkward in herself, working shifts in a kitchen bar and...

Hiding, Susie realised.

She'd been hiding even back then...

Only her rather pale and drab past wasn't the issue now, and she listened as Dante told her what had happened between him and Rosa.

'We both agreed it was to be a one-off.'

Never had Susie been more grateful for her reticence—for holding back and not automatically voicing her thoughts. It meant she hadn't jumped straight in and was able to speak in an unaccusatory tone.

'You were nineteen. So, they weren't married at the time?'

'God, no.'

He dismissed that as if he were brushing off a fly, and then he looked over at her. 'But it didn't end brilliantly. She suddenly seemed to think that our brief hook-up meant we were going out. That was never what we agreed.'

Susie fought not to react—not to show in her features that

she didn't like that term...*brief hook-up*. Not because of any moral code or such—she just didn't want it applied to her.

To them.

She didn't want what they'd found to be labelled as a 'hook-up'.

'So, for you it was just casual...?' Her voice tripped over the words. 'Like us? Like this?' she checked, speaking through lips that were possibly a little pale and taut.

But then she checked herself, doing her best to put her own issues with Dante aside—whatever they might be—and do her best to focus on him.

Dante looked at her and wanted to say, *It was nothing like us. Nothing like this...*

'We didn't do a lot of talking,' he said, and even as he answered he knew he'd said it all wrong.

Her short nails dug into his skin then, and she pulled her hand back as Dante continued.

'I told her from the start that I didn't want a relationship,' he said. 'I made it clear we were never going to be serious.'

'But she fell for you?'

'I don't know...'

Dante sat up in bed, his elbows on his knees, and Susie lay silent.

Susie didn't really know what to say, for as she looked at him, gorgeous in the morning light, on the bed still rumpled and warm from their time together, her body still thrumming from the breathtaking attention he'd given her, she could see both sides.

But contemplating how Rosa might have felt wouldn't be helpful right now—because no matter how sure and brave she'd been at the start, no matter that she'd sworn to hold on to her heart, when they said goodbye it was going to hurt.

Dante had seen her features change, could feel Susie's eyes on his back, and knew she was struggling to find the words to say.

He sat waiting for relief to come at having finally told someone.

Wasn't confession supposed to be good for the soul?

It didn't feel that way, and there was certainly no sense of relief.

He felt ill as he examined what he'd said, and even though Susie didn't press him for information, he carried on out loud. 'Rosa wanted to tell people about us,' he said. 'She kept calling...asking when I'd be back in Lucca...angling for me to take her to the ball. That would have been practically announcing our engagement...'

'So, she wanted to get serious?'

'Oh, yes—and I don't doubt her parents were behind it.' He turned and looked at Susie, still lying there, her eyes huge as they met his. 'They had big plans for their old shack of a winery.'

'What?' Her eyes snapped closed and her lips tightened. 'I've heard you be blunt before, but never mean...'

'Because I save it for those who deserve it.'

Dante shook his head and got out of bed. How the hell was he supposed to tell her all of it if he had to censor every word?

'Just because you hold everything in, it doesn't mean I have to,' he told her.

'Meaning?' she bristled.

'Just that.'

'I think you can say difficult things and still remain nice.'

'Fine,' Dante responded. 'I'll tell you *nicely*, then.'

And so he did. He gave her the cleaner, condensed version. 'I cut things off, and the rare times I was home I kept well away from Rosa, or even any conversation about her. Two years later I was walking on the walls when Rosa came running. She told me she and Sev were about to announce their engagement.'

'He didn't know that you'd slept together?'

'Of course not.'

'And you told him just before the wedding?'

'No,' he refuted. 'I tried to broach the subject... I said some things I perhaps shouldn't have.' He pursed his lips the way Susie had. 'Let's not go there. I'm sure you wouldn't approve.'

'Dante...'

Her eyes filled with tears and he could not bear to see them. He hated it that all he ever caused was hurt.

'Sev let me know my opinions were not welcome,' he told her.

'Dante...' She reached out to touch his shoulder, but he tensed and stood up.

'So there you have it.'

'What?'

'The worst action I have ever committed.'

He walked towards the shower, but she halted him with a question as he reached for the door.

'You mean sleeping with Rosa, or not telling Sev that you had?'

It was a very good question.

One he didn't answer.

Couldn't answer.

Instead, he climbed into the shower, and as the water hit him there was finally relief that he'd told her.

They'd been getting too close; he knew that very well.

Given Susie's reaction now, that would no longer be an issue.

That was the relief.

Dante was self-aware enough to know that in revealing the

truth he was effectively ending them. But better to cut things off now than be standing in a jewellers considering romantic gifts, or walking back into the bedroom and asking if she wanted to come to Milan.

No.

He didn't want anyone.

But even as the water cleansed him he felt contaminated— as if he brought nothing but despair into the lives of everyone who had ever mattered.

Susie knew she'd handled things badly.

As Dante showered she lay there for a while, knowing damn well that she'd been busy comparing their weekend of passion with what had happened between him and Rosa. And when he'd disparaged Rosa's family winery, she'd flinched. Not so much at what he'd said, more out of dread that one day she'd be similarly relegated to the past...a little footnote he referred to with derision because she'd been stupid enough to bare her heart.

She'd been shocked at first...worried that he'd been having an affair while Sev and Rosa were married. And when the relief of getting it wrong had hit her she'd been too involved in her own tumbled feelings to really listen to Dante, let alone say the right thing.

Now, as he came out of the shower, she just hoped it wasn't too late.

'Dante...'

'Let's leave it, hey?' His suggestion was kind. 'My car will be here soon. I don't want you leaving here upset.'

He said it nicely, but the implication was that it might be better for her to get dressed.

'I've thought about it,' Susie said. 'While you were in the shower.'

He shot her a slightly incredulous look. 'Oh? So do you have a solution?' He buttoned his shirt. 'I've been considering it for more than a decade.'

'Dante, please...' She felt like a plane that had been going round and around, attempting to land for a second time, only the conditions on the ground hadn't really improved. 'I think you should try telling Sev. It's been so many years. You've both lost so much. Could you write to him?' she suggested. 'Like your client did to his wife?'

'I am going to be dealing with the fallout of that letter today.' He looked at her then, and actually smiled. 'I've tried, believe me, but I can get never get past the first line... *"Dear Sev, sorry if this comes as a surprise..."'*

'He's your brother, though, and from everything I've heard you were once so close...' Her voice trailed off as he glanced out of the window.

'The car's here,' he told her. 'I can drop you off.'

Susie didn't want to get dressed, but she did.

She didn't want to leave, but she could hardly chain herself to the bed.

And she did not want to cry, but she felt very much as if she might.

'Hey...' Dante did not want it to end like this, and he took her in his arms. 'I shouldn't have told you.'

'I'm glad you did,' she told him.

'No, you're not,' he said gently.

He could see the doubt swirling in her eyes, feel the ache in her to fix something that was broken beyond repair.

And it was.

Of that he was certain.

But even if his car was waiting, and even if he might well

miss his plane, Dante chose to take the time to let Susie see just how impossible things were for him and Sev.

'Will you answer me something honestly?' Dante asked.

Susie gave a nervous laugh, a little worried as to what he might ask. 'Am I on the witness stand?'

'You are,' he said, and took her face in his hands.

It was just nice to be teased a little as they faced the difficult topic.

'We've had a good time,' he said. 'Agreed?'

'Yes…'

'And we're both clear that it should end neatly?'

'Yes.'

'With no hard feelings?'

She didn't answer quite so quickly then, because while there might not be hard feelings in the way he meant them, there were going to be difficult feelings—and certainly they'd hurt.

'Susie?' He was awaiting her response.

'No hard feelings,' she agreed—because she didn't regret what had taken place between them, nor ever would.

'Okay,' Dante said, and his hand moved to her arm. 'Now, what if in two years' time…?'

His hand paused, the fingers hovering over her arm, and she felt her skin goosebump, as if stretching to retain contact.

'What are the names of your sisters?' he asked.

'Cassandra and Celia.'

'Okay, what if Celia comes to visit, tells everyone she's met a guy, and she's hoping he'll propose this weekend…'

Susie's heart sank as she envisaged it.

'His name is Dante…'

She swallowed.

'And he's really good-looking,' he said, coaxing out a smile.

'Arrogant?' she checked.

'Absolutely,' Dante said. 'As well as brilliant in bed. Oh, and he's an attorney in Milan.'

Her smile faded then; this game was so hard to play.

'I don't know...' Her mind darted at the dreadful conundrum. 'I think I'd tell her.'

'What if I'd already met the rest of your family and told them we were getting engaged?'

'I...' Her certainty was gone.

And the more he spoke on, the more she didn't know.

'What if I then caught you alone and told you how much it would hurt your sister if you ever told her?'

'I'd probably do what you did...'

'And then I tragically die.'

Susie started to cry as she truly saw the hellish position he was in.

'Would you tell her then?' he asked. *"Hey, Celia, I never told you at the time, but before you were married Dante and I..."'*

'No.' She stopped him then. 'I would never tell her.'

'There you go.'

Susie stood still, wishing there was something better she could offer, and then she looked at Dante, a man who dealt in broken relationships for a living, and knew he would have examined every angle.

'I'm so sorry for what happened,' she told him.

'It's hardly your fault.'

'I *am* sorry, though; it must have been awful.'

He nodded.

'It still is?' Susie ventured.

He didn't answer; instead he gave her the nicest kiss.

But it was a slow and light kiss, a never-to-deepen kiss, and as they pulled apart Susie ran her tongue over her lips and they tasted of goodbye.

It was time to do this.

'I should go.'

She pulled on her boots and put her lip balm in her bag, and then she went to the bathroom and packed her toiletries in seconds. She came out as Dante was throwing a couple of last-minute things into his hand luggage.

'My driver just texted,' he said. His voice was a little husky, but then it wasn't even 6:00 a.m. 'I need a file…'

'I'll go,' she told him.

And there were no more kisses, no suggestions that they might meet again. She sort of waved at the door, but he was ramming a folder into his case, so she clipped down the stairs, pulled on her coat and collected her basket of goodies from the winery.

Dante closed his eyes as he heard the door close.

He'd seen the glittery tears in her eyes and he actually got it for once. Sometimes saying goodbye really was hard.

And he loathed how matter-of-fact he'd been, when he hadn't felt that way at all.

'*Merda,*' he said, cursing himself as he headed down the stairs.

To do what?

Call her back?

Take her back to bed and then say goodbye all over again?

He paused, saw her scarf on his banister and recalled removing it. He remembered their passion, their conversation, and everything in between.

He did not wrench open the door. Nor did he call her back to get her scarf and haul her into bed. Nor did he whisk her off to Milan.

Instead, he reminded himself of what he'd told his client.

Let her go with grace.

He put the scarf back over the banister and then went and collected his case. He headed out to the waiting vehicle and tried not to catch one final glimpse of Susie walking along the walls, carrying her basket…

CHAPTER EIGHT

ODDLY, WHEN IT felt as if the world was ending, she didn't cry. Instead, she greeted a couple of early-morning locals as if life was beautiful…as if the world was normal. There were even tiny buds on the trees that hadn't been there on Friday,

'*Mi scusi,*' someone said, and Susie smiled and stepped aside.

She was surprised at how calm she was, that she wasn't in floods of tears. But if anything, she was relieved.

Relieved that she hadn't burst out crying on him—or, worse, asked him when or if they might see each other again.

'*Permesso…*' a morning jogger scolded her.

But she barely noticed—was just relieved to make it to the apartment and climb the steps and be home.

'Hey…' Juliet smiled. 'Goodness, did you win a raffle?'

'I might have.' Susie smiled. 'Help yourself.'

'Seriously?' Louanna pounced on the offer, and was soon smearing truffled honey on crackers.

Oddly numb, Susie showered, tidied her room, caught up on a few calls, and then put on her uniform for work.

She was doing brilliantly, she decided. Over him already.

'Woo-hoo!' Louanna suddenly called from the lounge. 'Casadio!'

Frowning, Susie walked through—and there Dante was on her television screen.

'If I ever need to get divorced,' Louanna said, 'I am going to him.'

'What's it about?' Juliet asked.

'The divorce of the century,' Louanna said. 'Casadio is ruthless…he's trying to get a judge to agree to proceedings being delayed.'

Good grief!

Dante looked beautiful—as if he'd rolled over and gone to sleep after she'd left, and then been shaved and groomed by angels before stepping into a dark suit and his court robes.

'His robes…' Susie croaked—and then realised she'd said it out loud.

'*Toga,*' Louanna translated. 'They're in the Supreme Court.'

Dante even smirked as some journalist hurled a question at him.

Unlike his client, who walked alongside him, Dante was utterly calm, a little scathing, and completely immaculate.

He didn't even offer a 'no comment' as he walked from the court with his entourage, his *toga* billowing behind him.

Had she really been in bed with him just this morning?

She headed to work, bumping into a few more people along the way.

There was something fizzing inside her.

How could he be so completely fine?

Dante was far from fine.

There'd been an air of disorder when he'd arrived at work. As his client's letter had arrived while he was away, and an order had been broken, it meant he'd had no choice but to rock up to court.

And, no, the judge was not pleased at the stalling tactics—and no, there would be no more delays.

She'd glared at Dante. 'I don't like a circus outside my courtroom, Signor Casadio.'

And best of all, when he'd returned to his office, his head still spinning, Antonia had tried to bring him up to speed on lesser matters.

'This can surely wait?' Dante had said.

But Antonia liked a clear desk as much as he did, and had persisted. Relaying urgent messages, the names of other clients who were also about to stuff up, several requests from the press.

And now there was the personal stuff...

'Signor Adino, the jeweller...?'

'Dealt with.'

'Helene...' She glanced up, to confirm that he knew she meant his brother's PA. 'Helene would like to know if there is anything pressing regarding your trip home. She's more than happy to assist...'

Damn Sev. Too wrapped up in his own life to get on a plane himself, Dante thought. But now he wanted a full report.

He could wait.

'Oh, and a Susie Bilton left a message,' Antonia said. 'She said it was personal.'

'*Grazie,*' Dante said.

Merda, he thought.

Dante really didn't hear the rest, but he managed to nod in enough right places that finally he had the office to himself.

He'd tried to end it nicely this morning—had really thought she'd understood that there would be no repeats, no follow-up, no more...

He'd destroyed everyone he'd ever been close to, save for Gio, and he was not going to risk it with Susie.

Their weekend had been a rare one, and one to never repeat.

He'd been certain when he'd told Susie what had happened between him and Rosa that that would be it.

Now it was time to be his bastard self.

He dialled her number.

'Susie,' he said.

'Dante?'

'My assistant just informed me that you called.'

'Scusi...' she said, and he heard someone swear at her.

'Where are you?'

'Walking to work.'

'So why is someone swearing at you?'

He tried not to think of the last time he'd seen her walking on the walls. How he'd teased her about Mimi being Juliet...

Instead he got back to the point. 'And why did you call? Antonia said it was for personal reasons. I didn't think you were needy, Susie.'

'Needy?' She let out an incredulous laugh. 'I actually called you last Friday.'

'Why?'

'Because you told me I'd be able to find you in two minutes.'

He saw another image, this time of Susie standing under the umbrella.

'I didn't think you'd ever get the message or call me back.'

'Well, I have.'

'Just as well it wasn't a real emergency with your grandfather,' Susie said. 'It took you long enough.'

'What are you talking about?'

'I'm just pointing out that had there been a problem, you wouldn't have been around.'

'You're making no sense.'

Wasn't she? Susie asked herself as she was almost mowed down by a cyclist.

It finally registered that she was walking on the wrong side of the path. Possibly that was why everyone had been a little testy with her this morning.

'Susie...?' he said.

'I'm going to go,' Susie said, her voice a little high. 'I'm at work.'

Oh, she was fine.

Utterly fine.

If anything, she was angry. How dared Dante call her needy!

She stood there as Pedro allocated the team and told her the tables she was working.

'No bruschetta,' he said, and then told them everything else that was off the menu. 'We are short in the kitchen.'

Then he clapped his hands and everyone set off to work.

Except Susie.

'Problem, Susie?' Pedro said in English, as if she might not have understood his instructions. 'I said you're to work the bar tables and—'

'I understood what you said,' Susie said, in such a determined voice that, along with Pedro, she blinked in surprise. 'I'm so sorry, Pedro, I'll finish my shift, but after that I'm going to look for something else...'

He frowned.

'It's very disheartening to be told no without any consideration...to not be given even a chance...'

She was possibly saying what she wished she could say to Dante, Susie conceded, but Pedro would have to do. 'To be just written off.' She reached for her apron. 'Actually, I think I should just go home now.'

She marched to the little staff cloakroom, ready to go home, where she might take her scissors to that damn basket and tip the contents in the bin.

She halted and sat down on the small bench.

Oh, gosh, she wasn't okay.

Not at all.

She had been a public liability walking on the walls, and now she'd thrown in her job.

Oh—and now she understood what Dante had meant about walking around thinking you were being normal.

Then, at the thought of him out on the hills, searching, she started to panic, wondering how on earth she could get home without breaking down.

Never—not for a second—had she thought you could fall this hard for a person in a single weekend.

A single long weekend, she corrected.

A deliciously long and very wonderful weekend.

She'd never thought she was capable of this depth of feeling. It seriously hurt.

And it wasn't just her own pain she was dealing with. She seriously ached on his behalf too.

Gosh, she'd cried over her ex—but that had been more out of guilt for ending something that hadn't mattered enough.

Dante had made her feel like herself, feel important, feel wanted and adored and special. And he'd told her about Sev.

They'd shared so much…

'Susie?' There was a knock at the door and then Pedro put his head around it. 'You have a shift tonight in the kitchen,' he told her. 'Be here at four for prep.'

Thank goodness for work…

For exhilarating, exhausting shifts at the restaurant.

Now Susie wore the kitchen's huge black and white pants with a white top and apron. They were by far too big, but Susie loved them. And it was much easier to tackle mountains of tomatoes or onions than to address issues of the heart. And there was language classes and homework on top of that.

Susie was happy to collapse into bed each night and fall into an exhausted sleep.

It was in the silence of morning that she glimpsed despair and lay there so lonely, remembering how she and Dante would lie and talk…sometimes lying on their stomachs, facing each other, or on their backs looking over from their pillows…or the sheer pleasure of being held…

Then Juliet's violin would start!

Yes, she had every right to tell her to stop, but Juliet was apparently struggling at music school. As well as that, she was sweet and kind, and yesterday had even asked Susie if everything was okay.

Of course it was!

Work was increasingly brilliant. Soon she was no longer constantly chopping, and there were times when Cucou called her over and gave her a little demonstration, or asked her to taste something…

'My *sofrito*…' Cucou said now, speaking lovingly of the onion, celery and carrots he was frying in butter, and Susie's eyes were like a hawk's as she watched what he added.

Sofrito was the base for many Italian dishes, and every *nonna* and every chef guarded their own recipe. Parsley went in, she saw, and she noted the aromatics he added…

He gestured for her to try it and she took a little tasting stick. 'Oh, my…' she groaned at the sheer perfection. 'I need to add more butter to mine, and…' She looked at Cucou, who was smiling to himself, and was certain she hadn't seen all that he'd added. 'There's something else…'

He carried on stirring.

'Will I ever find out?'

'No.' Cucou shook his head. 'I shall take it to the grave.'

As well as work there were wonderful hours spent with Mimi—and not just walking on the walls. Sometimes they would go to the shops, or for coffee, and this gorgeous Saturday they were in Mimi's sister's home. Or was it Mimi's home? Susie still hadn't quite worked it out. But there they sat, going through old photos as Susie practised her Italian.

'This church is beautiful…'

'Very good,' Mimi approved, and turned a page in the album. 'Now say something about this photograph.'

'Goodness...'

It was a photo of a much younger Mimi, standing centre-stage in the amphitheatre. She was poured into velvet, her hair in ringlets, and clearly singing her heart out as the crowd watched spellbound.

'Look at you!'

'I was so beautiful that night...my voice soared.'

Mimi stretched her arms up like a ballerina and held the position as she recalled it, then gave a contented sigh as her hand came down. Susie wished she had a tenth of Mimi's fizz and confidence.

'I was singing for Eric,' she said, and smiled. 'He had asked me to the ball.'

'Are you hoping Gio will ask you?' Susie said, perhaps angling to know what was happening.

Apart from the little Dante had told her, it would seem he and Mimi were still living apart, although Mimi seemed a lot happier. In fact, she laughed now at Susie's question.

'Oh, no. The ball is very traditional. You only ever take one woman. It is different these days, but for some of us the tradition remains. Gio proposed to his beautiful wife there. It was where I met Eric...' She looked at Susie. 'You should go—Gio can get you invited!'

'I can't. My parents are visiting that weekend,' Susie said. 'As well as that, I don't have anyone to go with.'

She thought how dismissive Dante had been, even at the thought of inviting her. And although her thoughts darkened, she tried to lighten her tone.

'Anyway, I wouldn't have a clue what to wear. Let alone be able afford it.'

'I have a thousand gowns.' Mimi waved her excuses away. 'And I have been many sizes. Come.'

She took Susie upstairs to a gorgeous high-ceilinged room, with many full-length mirrors and an ornate dressing table with angled side mirrors.

'This is where I sing now, but it was once my dressing room,' Mimi said as she opened up what looked like an entire wall of wardrobes.

'Oh, Mimi…'

Susie stared at the array of beautiful gowns as Mimi pointed out some of the costumes she'd worn. Enchanted, Susie went through the dresses. Silks, velvets, frothy tulle of many shades and moods, vivid crimsons and sensual violets, as well as a dazzling russet. They were all labelled with the venues they'd been worn at, as well as the dates.

'Rosina,' Mimi sighed, taking out a black velvet dress. And perhaps she saw Susie's frown. 'I sang Rosina in *The Barber of Seville*.'

For a tiny second Susie had thought Mimi was talking about Rosa… Gosh, that last conversation…her last time with Dante. No matter how Susie filled her days, he was never more than a thought away.

Then came a brief diversion as her hand paused over a dusky gown. Susie wasn't sure if it was a pastel grey or pink, but the fabric was as soft as feathers to the touch.

'Oh!' Mimi gave a cry of delight, replacing her Rosina costume and coming over. 'What was I thinking? I actually hated that poor gown.'

'Why?'

'I usually prefer block colours. But this designer was famous for his achromatic designs and I wanted to own one. By the time it came to the final fitting I'd decided it was too subtle for me.' She put on her glasses and read her meticulous notes, then separated the layers of the skirt. 'The slip is Paris-pink, the chiffon a dove-grey.' She took it out and held it against Susie. 'I was very precious then—I believe I ended up wearing saffron.' She peered at the label again. 'It's never been worn. Try it.'

Susie couldn't resist, and slipped behind the curtains and undressed. Then she peered at the frothy gown wondering how to get it on. 'Do I...?'

'Step into it,' Mimi said from outside.

It felt like stepping into heaven. It was glorious, even allowing for the straps of her bra, and she stared at her image, a little pale and washed out, as Mimi chatted away.

'In Milan, I had four people helping me into it.'

Dante was in Milan...

That was all it took and he was back at the forefront of her mind. Gosh, no matter how Susie tried she could not keep thoughts of him at bay.

The curtain was swept back and Mimi stepped in. 'It's heavenly,' Susie said. 'Although even done up I think it'll be a bit too big...'

'It's corseted,' Mimi said. She instructed Susie to take off her bra, then took a little implement like a crochet hook to do up the back buttons. 'Arthritis,' she explained, and then, with not a jot of awkwardness, she stared at Susie in the mirror and jostled her breasts.

'Ow!' Susie said. 'That hurt!'

'I barely touched them!' Mimi laughed as she arranged the skirt and then looked at Susie's reflection. 'Oh, Susie...' She gave her verdict. 'It's perfect.'

'No, I think you were right about the colour,' she said. 'I do look pale in it.'

'Because you are pale,' Mimi said. 'This plays it up.'

Mimi lifted Susie's hair, as if trying to decide if it should be worn up or down.

'Please think about going...you'd be the belle of the ball.'

There was the sudden threat of tears. But Susie hadn't cried since she'd first torn off her apron and demanded a trial in the kitchen. And she was not going to cry now.

'It's gorgeous,' Susie said, 'but...' She shook her head. 'I really can't.'

'Surely your parents would love to see you all dressed up and enjoying yourself?'

'Not if they've flown over to see me!' Susie laughed, though it wasn't just the fact that her parents were coming that held her back. It was the thought of attending the ball alone when she'd have given anything to attend with Dante.

He hadn't messaged, and certainly there hadn't been any flowers.

Susie wondered if he even thought of her at all...

CHAPTER NINE

DANTE WAS DOING his level best not to think of Susie.

His vague plan to send her a gift and some flowers once the court case was over kept changing.

Perhaps a handwritten card, rather than one written by the florist...

But even that seemed too impersonal.

She had her parents visiting that weekend in the middle of his court trial, but perhaps he'd send something after that?

Then he would snap himself out of it, tell himself that the hollowed-out feeling he seemed to have acquired since he'd returned to Milan would be gone by then.

Certainly there was enough work to bury himself in. Both the client and his soon-to-be ex-wife seemed determined to have their day in court, and there were plenty of other clients...

And there was always family.

'Dante!'

Gio was sounding chirpy this morning, and had been for several mornings prior. Dante was starting to rue the day he'd showed him how to use that smart phone.

'Hey, Gio,' Dante said. 'How are you?'

'Good,' Gio said. 'I know we spoke yesterday, but I have good news—Mimi and I are getting married.'

'Congratulations.' Dante found that he was smiling. 'Did she like her ring?'

'She's not wearing it until the wedding. We want to keep it very small; most people can find out about it once we're married. Just you and Sev... Mimi's sister...'

'When are you looking at?' Dante asked, pulling up his calendar.

'Valentine's Day.'

'Gio...' Dante frowned. 'That's two days away. You mean next Valentine's Day?'

'I'm eighty-four, Dante,' Gio snapped. 'Of course I don't mean next year.'

Dante screwed his eyes closed in exasperation. He had honestly thought any wedding would be a couple of months away, when Susie had gone.

'Gio, I have that big case commencing next week.'

'That is why we are doing it before. It is just a lunch. Are things so bad between you and Sev that you cannot stand to be in the same room for my wedding?'

'Don't be ridiculous.' He pushed out a lighter tone, while squeezing the bridge of his nose between thumb and forefinger. 'Of course I shall be there...' He asked the question he wasn't sure he wanted the answer to. 'Where is the lunch to be?'

'At home. Mimi insists on cooking for us.'

Dante found there wasn't the expected wave of relief that there would be no encounter with Susie at Pearla's...

'I have eaten rather a lot of restaurant food lately.' Gio laughed.

'Are you still getting home deliveries from Pearla's?' Dante had tried not to ask before, but today he couldn't help but delve.

'Sometimes.' Gio laughed. 'Mimi refuses to move back in till after the wedding, so I order now and then—but not as much. Things changed.'

'What changed?'

'Susie stopped bringing my meals. And I miss her a lot.'

God, so did he.

The hollowed-out feeling he'd had since he returned to Milan had morphed into a black hole of regret that felt as if it might consume him.

'She's working in the kitchen now,' said Gio.

'Oh?' Dante said, as if it meant little to him. But he stood from his seat and started to pace as realisation dawned.

Susie would be in Lucca.

And not just for Gio's wedding.

She didn't need to go on that course in Florence. She was working in the kitchen of one of the best restaurants in Italy. Which meant every time he returned, Susie would be there.

'Dante? About the wedding…'

Gio brought him back to the reason for his call.

'We are not going to let anyone know—not until the wedding papers are signed.'

'I understand.' The whole town would be there otherwise. 'I'm so happy for you both.'

'Two brides to your zero!' Gio laughed. 'My love life is better than yours.'

'It is.'

'But if you want to bring a guest,' Gio said. 'Someone special…'

Of course he would like to bring a guest. How much easier the day would be with Susie by his side. It would make facing Sev a whole lot easier. But he was not about to use Susie as a shield.

And, of course he wanted to call Susie tell her he was returning for one night…perhaps arrange to see her after the wedding.

But that would set a dangerous precedent.

'No,' he told his grandfather. 'It will just be me.'

Susie had never really been one for Valentine's Day. And Lucca was such a romantic city that it seemed to ram home her loss as the big day approached.

Museums were holding special events and there were beautiful floral displays everywhere. Pearla's was booked out for both lunch and dinner, with Cucou planning a special menu...

Was it the same in Milan? Susie pondered as she awoke on the dreaded day. Were there red roses by the fountains? Was there so much romance in the air that Dante would pause and finally think of her? Would flowers finally arrive from him today?

She lay listening to Juliet playing. It was a different piece than usual, and actually rather beautiful. It made her think of Dante, although that wasn't unusual. Everything did these say.

She checked her phone, chiding herself for vague hope, while knowing damn well he wouldn't call now...

It had been weeks of nothing and she knew his big case started on Monday—no doubt he was busy working, or out with some gorgeous beauty who understood that when Dante said he didn't get involved he meant it.

As she did most Saturdays, she called home.

'How are you, darling?' Mum was sounding cheerful.

'Busy,' Susie said. 'One more week till you come. You need to tell me your flights...' She scrambled for a pen. 'I'm really looking forward to seeing you.'

'And we're excited to see you too—but I'm afraid it's not going to be until April.'

'Sorry?'

'The twins' move has been brought forward. They're moving that weekend.'

Susie felt her heart plummet as she was told how they needed Dad to shift some heavy stuff...how there was simply no other day...

'But, Mum...' Susie tried to quash her wail of despair. 'I've booked the days off.'

'I know you have, darling,' Mum said. 'But their landlord

wanted tenants in immediately, and they'd have lost the flat otherwise. You know that we'd do the same for you…'

Actually, Susie didn't!

'But it's my birthday…'

'Susie!'

Mum gave a little laugh—the one that she always used to warn her that she was being petty. And possibly she was. It wasn't a milestone birthday…it didn't actually matter…

Except it did.

She wanted one birthday where it was all about her.

One cake that was her own, and not just another candle stuck in beside the twins' double ones, which always seemed to shine so much more brightly.

'Susie, we *are* coming—it just won't be next week.'

'Mum, please—'

'Now, stop being silly!' Mum gave her little warning laugh again. 'You sound as if you're jealous.'

'I am.'

'Pardon?'

'I am jealous,' Susie confirmed. 'I'll call you next week. Bye.'

Ending the call, she took a breath and waited for guilt or panic to arrive. But bizarrely she felt a bit better for having said it.

She went into the kitchen and smiled at Louanna, who was dressed in black. *'Buongiorno…'*

'There's coffee in the pot,' Louanna said.

'Are you working?' Susie asked.

'It's Valentine's Day in Lucca—there's a lot of love and music to be made.'

She looked up as Juliet came in. She was also dressed in black, her red hair up in a chignon and pearls in her ears, clearly in for a busy day also.

'But no love for us today...' Louanna sighed. 'We just get to watch other people be romantic. I'll get packed up.'

'I didn't wake you, did I?' Juliet asked as Louanna went to sort out her cello.

'I was up anyway,' Susie said, and smiled, deciding not to take her grumpy mood out on everyone else. 'You sounded incredible.'

'"*Una Ve Poco Fa*",' Juliet said. '"A Voice I Once Heard". It's a gorgeous piece.' Then perhaps she saw the strain on Susie's face. 'Are you okay?'

'Of course.' Susie nodded, then shrugged. 'I just found out my parents aren't coming next week.'

'I'm sorry... I know you were so looking forward to it. You've been quiet for a while, though, and you are very pale.'

Susie saw a flicker of concern in Juliet's eyes and did not want it to be there. Juliet didn't know about Dante, no one did.

'I'm honestly fine. It's just the new job, all my course work...'

'If you ever want to talk?' Juliet offered, before she and Louanna headed out.

Susie didn't know how she felt, let alone what she might say.

It wasn't Juliet's early practice sessions, nor was it even that her parents were no longer coming.

She kept waiting to feel okay—to wake up and know she was over Dante.

It was the first time she'd been alone in the flat in for ever. Mimi was busy today, so there would be no walking on the walls. And, yes, she had homework for class, but for now it could wait.

Two minutes into her peaceful moment her phone rang.

It wasn't Dante.

And it wasn't her mum, saying she'd thought about it and they were coming next week after all.

Nor was it a florist staggering under the weight of red roses, calling to be buzzed in…though she briefly flared with hope.

'Susie!' It was a frantic Pedro. 'Can you come in early and help with prep? We have a function—a last-minute booking.'

'Sure.'

'And I know you won't be happy, but after prep we need you to do some waitressing…'

'Pedro…' She did not want this, but of course it was a feeble protest. Her apron-flinging moment had been a brief one. 'When do you want me to come in?'

'Now.'

Even though Pearla's wasn't yet open, the restaurant was hectic on this special day. The pastry chefs were all frantic, and Cucou barely looked up—just pointed her to a mountain of parsley.

'Prep that, then help Phillipe with the *arancini*.'

But, as busy as it was, Cucou still found time to teach.

'Susie…?' He called her over and she gazed upon his *sofrito*—buttery, silky, salty perfection. 'Do you see the gloss?'

'Yes…'

She put in her tiny little spatula and took a taste, and then she looked at Cucou, about to tell him she knew his secret, for she could taste anchovies.

'Good, yes?' he asked.

'Perfect.' Susie nodded.

Certainly she wasn't about to disagree with Cucou, and she was grateful when Phillipe came over and tasted it too.

'To die for!' he declared.

'Are you waitressing at the wedding?' Cucou asked her.

'Is it a wedding?'

He nodded. 'If so, the cake needs to come out of the chiller exactly twenty minutes before serving—no earlier…' Cucou gave her some more somewhat unusual instructions, and perhaps saw her frown. 'It's a tiny wedding…just a party of five…'

Cucou opened up the massive chiller, and if this Valentine's Day had proved challenging for Susie so far, it suddenly became impossible.

Gio and Mimi

The names were piped on the cake elaborately, and there were little hearts and bells… And if there was a God, then he was playing tricks on her, surely?

'Gio and Mimi are getting married?' she croaked, hurt that Mimi hadn't told her. 'When?'

Cucou glanced at the huge clock. 'About now…'

He closed the box on the precious cake.

'Susie…?' Pedro called. 'You need to get changed.'

As she headed for the cloakroom she braced herself for a second hurt.

Dante.

Dante won't even be there, Susie told herself as she slipped on her stockings and wriggled into her black dress, remembering his hands on the zip even as she reached for it. Remembering his hands on her hips and how in that moment their promised one night had turned into three…

Of course he'll be there, she argued silently in her mind as she put on her ugly sensible shoes and then tied her black apron on.

And if he was going to be in Lucca then he'd want to see her, surely?

Call her?

Warn her so she could at least warn her heart!

But then what did one weekend with a waitress mean to a man like Dante?

He'd made her feel special and adored, but she didn't doubt he'd done the same to many women.

He wouldn't be here, she reassured herself as she tied her hair into a low bun and put a slick of lipstick on.

It felt odd to step into Gio's through the staff entrance and not the main kitchen.

Pedro was his usual self—behind the scenes he was frantic, but she knew he would be all polished smiles when the wedding party arrived.

'Susie and Camilla, you are here in the butler's kitchen, serving...'

'Can't I work in the main kitchen?' Susie asked.

'You're a waitress today,' Pedro reminded her sharply.

Oh, God.

She would like to run...go and hide in the lovely garden and drag in some air. Instead she walked through to the private dining room, where the table was being hastily dressed for a very elegant wedding breakfast—more candles, of course, as well as silver-framed photos on occasional tables. To her surprise Juliet and Louanna were there, as well as a tall gentleman— obviously their conductor—and a harried-looking older lady.

'Susie...' Juliet called.

She gave a quick wave. Now and then they'd worked the same venue, but there was no time to stop now. They were busy tuning up, and Susie was busy accepting platters from the main kitchen.

Then she was directed by Pedro to hold a champagne tray at the door.

'Wait...' the conductor was saying, and Susie couldn't work it all out—because surely there was no such thing as a surprise wedding?

Yet there was Mimi, looking stunning in an emerald gown, giving a shocked gasp as she stepped into the dining room.

'Gio!' She laughed, and kissed the groom as the music started.

Susie stood still as hands reached for the champagne flutes

on the tray she held. No matter how she tried not to notice, she knew which hand was Dante's.

'*Grazie*, Susie,' he said.

'You're welcome.'

Mimi was still happily protesting. 'This is beautiful…but I wanted to cook for my wonderful husband, my new family.'

'You think I would have you cooking on your wedding day?' Gio was delighted as he held a chair for his bride. 'Sit, my love.'

'I am not going to sit,' Mimi said. 'I have to *sing*.'

'Great…' the other man in the party said under his breath as he took a drink from Susie's tray. 'That's all we need…'

Susie looked up to get her first glimpse of Sev. His comment had clearly been to himself rather than to Susie. In fact, he didn't even deign to spare her a glance—just took a glass and raised it.

The music paused as Mimi smiled to her small audience and then looked at her husband.

'My love gets stronger every day…my voice not so much. Forgive me…'

'You have the voice of an angel,' Gio said.

Mimi looked towards the string quartet. '"*Una Voce Poco Fa*"? "A Voice I Once Heard…"'

It was the piece Juliet had been practising this morning, Susie realised. Perhaps Gio had told them it was Mimi's favourite?

There was silence, then a short musical introduction, and then Mimi reached out her hand towards her new husband, and for the first time Susie heard her glorious voice.

Susie knew nothing about opera, and hadn't really understood before how a song might know exactly how she felt—how a song might mirror the aching desire and the loneliness that had suffocated her since her parting from Dante.

God, she missed him so much…

As the song neared its conclusion Susie dared to look over, but of course Dante was looking at Mimi.

At first, she couldn't read his features. His chin was up, his lips slightly taut, and for the first time she saw that the very smooth Dante appeared slightly awkward.

'Bravo,' he said as Mimi finished.

Possibly it was to do with his brother being there, because there was no hint of awkwardness when he came into the little butler's kitchen a while later.

'I didn't know Gio was getting lunch catered here,' Dante explained. 'When he told me about the wedding he said it was just a family lunch and Mimi was cooking. The string quartet and the private lunch was a last-minute thing, apparently.'

'Good for Gio.' Susie pushed out a smile, not wanting to make a fuss. After all it was a very special day.

And it wasn't the wedding that hurt.

She understood why Mimi hadn't said anything; it was clearly a very intimate affair. What hurt was the fact that Dante had known he'd be in Lucca and hadn't even thought to call.

Clearly she was *nothing*.

'Susie?' He caught her wrist. 'I had no idea you'd be here.'

The first time he'd held her arm her skin had prickled with goosebumps, perhaps unsure how to react to a delicious stranger. Now, though, her body knew the pleasures his touch was capable of, and it flared in reaction. She looked up to those dark eyes, and down to the full, sensual mouth that she'd missed so much, and almost stepped forward to kiss him.

No!

She wasn't going to be caught kissing Dante in the butler's kitchen. He couldn't just pick up where he'd left off.

'I'm at work, Dante.' She wrenched her arm away and stepped back.

'I was just attempting to explain...'

He stopped when Mimi burst into the kitchen.

'Susie!' Mimi pulled her into a hug. 'I was *desperate* to tell you.' She held out her hand. 'But I knew if we told a soul...'

Dante left them, and Susie examined Mimi's stunning ring—reds, violets, greens, encircled with diamonds.

'It's a rare black opal,' Mimi said. 'Gio says it is for the colour I bring to his life.'

It was a very long, very gorgeous lunch, and thankfully the happy couple were so besotted they didn't seem to notice the strain between the two brothers—or perhaps they were used to it by now.

The speeches were short and informal.

'Mimi, you have brought so much happiness to Gio...' Sev smiled at his new step-grandmother, then looked at his grandfather. 'Gio, you deserve every happiness.'

'You do too,' Gio said, dabbing his eyes.

It was far from effusive, yet Susie could feel the love in the room, and she found she was holding her breath as Dante stood to make his toast.

'Mimi...' he said. 'It is wonderful to share in this day, to know you are now part of our family.' He looked to his grandfather. 'And Gio...'

He paused.

He really paused, and Susie felt her throat squeeze tight.

'We love you...'

Gio nodded. 'I love you boys too.'

The music recommenced, and Susie headed back to the main kitchen to take out the cake. She nodded when Pedro suggested she take a break.

'There's some lunch for you in the kitchen.'

Susie didn't fancy it, though, and just took a couple of *arancini* balls in a napkin.

'I might just go out to the garden,' she told him.

'Go through the side entrance,' he said, and nodded.

She slipped out and walked under the portico. It was a

lovely chilly day, and it was nice to be cold for a moment, and to let a tear slip out. But she hastily wiped it away when she saw Dante had come out too.

'There you are…' He stood over her. 'Gio said you were working in the kitchen now. Congratulations.'

'Thanks, although I'm waitressing today—oh, and tonight.' She looked up, took in his lovely suit. She had sort of known he'd come out—or rather she'd hoped he might. 'How's your client? The one with the letter?'

'Driving me crazy. Court on Monday.' He rolled his eyes. 'I don't think either party is ready. The judge is right, I fear—it's going to be a circus.'

Dante wasn't outside by chance. He knew how awkward this wedding must be for Susie, but he'd been resisting calling her for weeks.

Resisting…

He glanced back at the restaurant. 'Mimi's going to sing again.'

'I think that's beautiful.'

'Maybe…but I get embarrassed when people sing to each other.'

'You!'

'I don't know why… I always have.' He couldn't help but smile as he took a seat on the bench beside her. 'Just my luck to now be related to someone who does it all the time.'

Susie couldn't help but laugh, and then she thought about Sev's comment. 'You should tell Sev—I don't think he's too keen on the singing either.'

She glanced over at his grim expression. 'Please…listen… I thought about what you said. If it was you and Celia… You're right, I wouldn't tell her.'

'No?'

'I think I'd lose her if I did...' She was being honest, and it hurt, but it was true.

'So why do you think I should tell Sev?'

'If it was Cassie who'd slept with you, though...'

'They're identical twins.' He frowned in confusion.

'I mean if you took me out of the scenario—if it was just between them—well, I think she'd forgive her, or they'd somehow get past it, because they love each other and they'd work it through.'

'It's not as straightforward as that.'

'You could try?'

Susie honestly expected him to stand up and stalk off, but he didn't.

'Rosa told me she thought she might be pregnant.'

He snapped it out, as if it was something he'd never wanted to share.

'Do you think Sev would want to hear that?'

'I don't know...' Her voice shivered. 'Was she?'

'Of course not.' He looked around and made certain there was no one else about. 'She kept calling, asking me when I'd be home—that sort of thing. I reminded her we weren't a couple. Then she called and said she was late...that maybe the condom had broken. I knew it had not.'

'Accidents happen...'

'Not to me. I knew I'd been careful; I knew she was lying. I flew straight back—she wasn't expecting me to. I called her and asked to meet immediately. I said that she should see a doctor and that I'd come with her. She didn't want that, of course.'

'What did she want?'

'Marriage,' he said flatly. 'She suggested I go and speak with her parents and make things "respectable" before anyone caught on...' His laugh was black. 'I told her there wasn't a chance in hell I'd marry her, and that I'd want a DNA test before we spoke any further. Look, I'm not proud of how I reacted, but I was certain she was lying.'

'Why would she lie?'

'Why?' Dante repeated. 'Because she was trying to set me up—no doubt at the urging of her parents. There have been fights over this land for generations...the De Santis family have always wanted the wineries merged.'

'You really think she was doing that?'

'Susie, I spend half my working life sorting this kind of issue out. Family lines, succession, mergers of land... I didn't get interested in that side of the law by chance.'

Susie exhaled shakily.

'I told her she should take a test right there and then. I went and bought one.' He gave a mirthless laugh. 'By the time I got back from the pharmacy, lo and behold, she told me it had been a false alarm.'

'Her period had arrived?'

'Of course.'

'You never told anyone?'

'I wish to God I'd told my brother, but I didn't.' The regret in his voice turned to bitterness. 'A couple of years later I was visiting home, walking on the walls, and she came running after me crying, telling me that she and Sev were in love, that he must never find out about us. I thought she must have pulled the same stunt that she tried with me and told him she was pregnant. Sev's a lot more dutiful than me—or he was... I tried to talk to him a couple of times, but he just blocked me... On the eve of the wedding I was more direct. I said that if she was saying she was pregnant, it was no reason for him to marry her. Sev hit me—told me never to speak of Rosa like that. He said he loved her...'

'Do you think he did?'

'Who knows with Sev? I stayed back... I figured if he

wanted to talk…' He shook his head. 'Then the accident happened. I tried to talk to him again, but he didn't want to hear it.'

'He might now.'

'No.' He looked over to where she sat. 'I've thought about your question…if I regret sleeping with Rosa, or not telling Sev.'

'And?'

'I wish I'd never laid eyes on her.' He stood. 'Sev and I are finished.'

He headed back to the party and Susie just sat there for a moment. Then glanced at the time and knew she had to head back.

Dante watched Susie leave the private dining room and saw her pass the west side windows. He tried to focus on something Mimi was saying, and to tell her he wanted to leave discreetly.

But no…

That would not be fair.

And when Susie returned—when the cake had been cut and the catering staff were packing up—he wanted to go into the kitchen and kiss her neck…turn her in his arms and lose himself in her for a moment.

But that would not be fair either.

'Dante?'

Sev was trying to be polite, for the sake of the wedding, and held up a bottle of whisky. Dante nodded, but he could see the hell in his brother's eyes even as he attempted to be civil and knew he'd caused so much of it.

Then Mimi took the microphone again. Briefly he met Sev's eyes and gave a small smile, one only the brother who knew him very well might understand.

Only Sev didn't return the smile, and Dante looked away.

God, but he wanted Susie…

Dante gave in then—pushed back his chair and walked

into the kitchen. But it was empty, and everything was neat and tidy.

The staff were gone.

It was just family now.

Two feuding brothers, whisky and wine.

Oh, and music that was set to play late into the night.

What could possibly go wrong?

It was after Mimi's sister had left that Gio turned his attention to his grandsons.

The musicians still played softly; his grandfather's conversation was getting louder the later the hour.

'Dante, why don't you ever bring someone?' Gio demanded, seeming determined to sort out his grandson's love life.

Dante strummed his fingers on the table and gave a noncommittal smile.

Right now, he wished he had.

He kept thinking of Susie, and how he'd stalked off in the garden that day, after he'd told her everything.

'And you...?' Gio turned his inappropriate questions to Sev. 'Why are you staying in a hotel when you have a home here?'

'It is your honeymoon,' Sev quipped.

'Then why not stay at your brother's?' Gio persisted. 'Always you stay in a hotel...'

'I might want to find company.'

'Then bring her along.'

Sev gave a wry laugh and rolled his eyes, and then Mimi decided it was time to treat them all to another performance.

'Ah, I know!' Mimi said, and delivered her choice to the ensemble.

The violinists and viola player took up their bows, but the cellist abruptly glanced towards Sev. She was local, and knew this was perhaps not the best choice.

A beautiful soprano aria by Puccini. They were in Lucca,

after all—his birthplace. So possibly it was a natural choice, and Mimi would have performed it often…

Except it had been sung at Sev and Rosa's wedding.

As well as at Rosa's funeral.

Gio didn't seem to remember—he was gazing at his bride. Dante closed his eyes for a moment, then opened them to look at Sev, who was as white as marble, though there was clearly still some blood supply, given the muscle leaping in his cheek.

Mimi's voice seemed to be wrapping around them both, taking them back to those dreadful days.

'Mimi…' Dante went to halt her, but Sev told him to leave it, and so they sat through the hellish performance and briefly met each other's eyes. Sev's look was less than friendly as his gaze lifted to Dante's scar.

'Bravo,' Sev said at last, and stood and gave Mimi a burst of applause. 'Now, I really do have to go.'

'Not yet!' Mimi pouted, but thankfully Gio suddenly seemed exhausted and ready for guests to leave.

'And me.' Dante stood.

Sev was out in a matter of moments, so it was Dante who bore the brunt of the farewell hugs and kisses, but soon he was up on the walls, chasing his brother down.

'Sev!' he called out.

Sev told him to back off, only Dante ignored him.

When he'd caught up, Sev told him to back off again—only rather less politely.

'No!' Dante grabbed him. 'Listen to me. I should never have said what I did. I get it, okay? And I am sorry. But it's been almost ten years.'

'I said leave it,' Sev warned, and now he had Dante by the lapels of his jacket. 'Or I'll take care of the other eye. See how good you look in court on Monday then. Go to hell, Dante.'

'We're brothers.'

'Correction,' Sev said, and shoved him. 'We used to be!'

Dante walked off.

Possibly because he knew he had court on Monday...

More likely it was guilt.

For whatever reason he walked away, arriving home to an empty house, and the coral scarf Susie had left behind still draped over the banister.

He'd be having words with his housekeeper, Dante decided, picking up the long strip of coral silk and pressing it to his face, inhaling her scent, unable to resist any more.

The worst Valentine's Day ever!

Susie's knew that her long shift might be worth it come payday, but seeing Dante had been hell, and then serving happy couples late into the night...

She was utterly spent—more exhausted than she could ever recall being.

One more week of language school and hopefully then things would get easier.

There was no Dante waiting with ice cream when she stepped out of Pearla's—not that she wanted one. If anything, the thought made her feel a little bit ill.

Susie stopped mid-stride, a few throwaway thoughts starting to merge in her mind. There was a flutter of panic in her chest.

She walked more briskly, telling herself she was being ridiculous.

She'd missed one pill.

Or two.

Her breasts hurt...

Because she was getting her period.

She'd told herself that when she'd been trying on Mimi's gowns.

'Hey...'

The one time she hadn't been hoping, Dante was here!

He'd been leaning against the wall of the ancient apartment block, but stood up straight when he saw her.

'Shouldn't you be at the wedding?' she asked.

'It was time to go.' He gave a grim flash of a smile. 'Can we talk inside?'

'I'm not sure if my flatmates are in.'

'What? Aren't you allowed to bring men back to the nunnery?'

He must have seen from her expression that his little joke wasn't well received, and perhaps he thought he knew the reason, because he said, 'Susie, I had no idea you'd be there today. I was...'

'So you were just going to fly in and fly out? Not even...?'

Dante looked as if he hadn't had the best night either. 'I have a home here in Lucca—am I to you inform you every time I'll be home?'

'Of course not.'

'Did you want that?' he asked. 'Did you want me to call you and say, *I'll be here for one night. I can't tell you why, but can I come over?*'

'No.'

She shook her head; she hadn't thought of it like that. No, she didn't want to be his on-call mistress.

'So what? Now that I know you're here, you thought you'd drop in?'

'If you'd let me finish... I was trying to say I had no idea you'd be there today, but I was pleased you were.'

Her head was still spinning—not just from seeing him, but at the possibility that she might be pregnant, and also...

She looked at Dante and realised that there was another problem.

It would be hell to be pregnant by the playboy attorney...

But to love him...?

As if to deny her own want, she snapped, 'What do you want, Dante?'

'This.'

He kissed her then—a fervent and deep whisky-laced kiss that tasted delicious—and she was in his arms, kissing him back with passion. Hurling herself at the exit that was Dante, desperate for escape from her thoughts.

His hands were everywhere, and Susie truly wished they were at his house. There they could fall through the door and be completely alone...

But then she hauled herself back.

It was only a temporary escape.

She pulled her head back, peeled her body from his. 'You'd better go.'

'Susie...' He took a breath and then released her. They stood apart for a moment, and Dante seemed to gather his thoughts.

'Can we talk?' he asked.

'Talk?' she scoffed.

'Yes,' he said. 'Please.'

She was still reeling, though. She knew they would end up in bed, and that she'd be in love with him just a little bit more.

In love and possibly pregnant by a man who couldn't commit to anything.

And so she'd give him a chance to talk.

One chance.

'I spoke to my mother this morning...' she told him.

He frowned. Clearly he had no idea what she was getting at.

'The twins are moving house next weekend, so they're not visiting me now till April.'

He frowned again.

'It means I'll be free on my birthday weekend. The weekend of the ball. You could come.'

'I'll be in the middle of a court case.'

It wasn't the answer she wanted. She wanted him to understand how much it hurt that her parents had cancelled visiting her on her birthday, for him to fix it, to tell her not to worry.

To tell her they were about more than sex.

But, as charming as he could be, he didn't step in—and he didn't wave a wand and say, *Susie, you shall go to the ball.*

'What are you saying here, Susie? If I ask you to the ball then I get to come upstairs?'

Susie flushed. 'I didn't mean it like that.'

'No...' He shook his head. 'You want to use me in whatever strange competition you have going on with your sisters.'

'I might be in competition with them,' Susie retorted, 'but I'd rather that than throw in the towel as you have with Sev.'

Dante abruptly turned and walked off.

And, as he did so he raised his arm as if he was doing just that—throwing in the towel on them.

Damn...

Susie ran up the stairs and wanted to immediately run down again. Instead she sat on the couch and buried her head in her hands.

Oh, she knew she'd handled that terribly. But the shock of seeing him two seconds after she'd realised she might be pregnant...

'Susie?'

It was Juliet, carrying two boxes of pizza, with Louanna behind her.

'You missed all the fun,' Louanna said.

'It wasn't fun—it was awful,' Juliet groaned.

'The Casadio brothers...' Louanna said with glee.

Susie's heart sank. 'What happened?' she asked.

'Mimi sang *"O Mio Babbino Caro"*,' Juliet said, sinking down on a chair. 'You should have seen the look that passed between the two brothers.'

'And...?'

'Apparently it was played at the older brother's wedding,'

Louanna explained. 'And I think it might have been played at the wife's funeral too. I thought Sev was about to explode... Then apparently there was a fight on the walls.'

'No...' Juliet shook her head, and told her the gossip she'd heard while getting pizza.

Only Susie wasn't listening.

She closed her eyes in wretched regret for her handling of things.

Dante really had wanted to talk.

And kiss...

It was the worst Valentine's Day ever.

CHAPTER TEN

'How was class?' Juliet asked Susie when she came in on Monday.

'Great,' she said, but her voice was rather flat as she joined her flatmate in the lounge.

Juliet didn't look so great either. She was sitting staring at the muted television and looked as if she'd been crying.

'Don't you have rehearsals?' asked Susie.

'No, I wasn't selected to play for the ball.'

Susie knew how that felt. 'I'm sorry.'

'I'm worried about my scholarship,' Juliet admitted. 'I'm not keeping up. I'm working at the store and the bar to pay my rent, and there just aren't enough hours to practise. I'm getting up at the crack of dawn...trying to cram things in...'

Susie moved over to Juliet's couch and gave her a hug. She was pleased that in this instance she hadn't said anything to Juliet about the noise.

'Can your family help?' she asked.

'God, no.' Juliet shook her head. 'I'm not giving up my music, but I do have to face things.' Then she paused and looked at the television screen. 'There he is...'

Susie tried not to turn her head too quickly, and attempted to feign nonchalance as she saw Dante, looking utterly together, walking towards the court.

'That's from this morning,' Juliet said. 'Clearly he wasn't in a fight—Louanna's such a gossip.'

Dante wore a dark grey suit and a dark gunmetal tie, and his white shirt almost gleamed in the mid-morning light. He looked a whole lot better than Susie.

The footage ended and the scene flicked back to the court, where all the cameras were waiting for news outside.

Juliet spoke again. 'It was a difficult wedding.'

Susie tore her eyes away from the screen. 'I thought it was gorgeous.'

'Of course—but it was so sad. All those pictures every-where…and so many pieces we were told not to perform. And then Mimi…'

Susie closed her eyes and felt so selfish. She'd been think-ing only of how hard it was for her. And that was what she regretted.

Dante had needed her, and instead of being there for him, or properly listening, she'd been angling for an invitation to the ball.

Then there was the sound of footsteps on the stairs and then the door opened and an excited Louanna rushed in. 'Turn the sound on!'

'What?'

'There's about to be a press conference.' She was unmuting the television. 'They're back together,' Louanna said. 'Again!'

The happy couple were smiling and holding hands, with their lawyers standing beside them, a little grim-faced, as a short statement was read.

'The past year has been difficult for both parties, who deeply regret getting third parties involved. They look for-ward to renewing their vows and moving forward.'

'See?' Louanna said. 'Only the lawyers win.'

Dante gave a short response and said he was pleased for his client and wished the couple well. He offered a tight smile, then shook his client's hand and walked back to his office, the rebuke from the judge still ringing in his ears.

'This case should never have made it to court, Signor Casadio.'

Once again, he was the bastard...

For two days he dealt with the press, with his staff, with the paperwork that had piled up, and then he went to his safe and took out a small envelope.

'I'm taking the rest of the week off,' he informed his PA.

Dante returned to his stunning apartment, and thought Susie was right—he could rent it out tomorrow, as a luxurious furnished penthouse, and apart from clothes and toiletries there was little he would have to take out...

He opened up the envelope and stared at the two small rubies in his palm. Again he recalled his mother with the jeweller, insisting on the stones she liked.

'Rubies...'

'Not diamonds?'

'I have so many diamonds...rubies are more beguiling...'

Then he remembered going back with his father.

'Just rubies?' he had checked.

'Si,' Signor Adino had said. *'She wants rubies only for her eternity ring.'*

Dante had turned to Sev. *'What's an eternity ring?'*

Now he remembered his response.

'Something infinite,' Sev had said. *'For ever.'*

But Dante had frowned.

'Even after you die?'

Dante had had a heart back then. He'd loved everyone so much. And at the thought of his *mamma* dying, Papa too, he'd started to cry.

'What have you said to him?' Papa had come over to them. *'Dante,'* he'd scolded. *'Stop.'*

Now Dante found he couldn't stop.

He hadn't cried at their death, nor at their funeral. Certainly he hadn't cried when Sev had hit him, nor at the needle going in and out as he'd been stitched up. Nor when he'd walked away from his life.

The day when Rosa had run up to him on the walls, pitched him against his brother, he'd muted all feelings.

Only since Susie had appeared had they started to return.

He thought of her in Lucca, happy in her new job. There was too much damage there, too much left undone, and the foundations were too shaky for him to even think of returning.

Instead, he looked again at the rubies and took out his phone.

'Signor Adino...'

A gift, Dante decided. And then he'd let her go.

'Are you still sulking, Susie?'

Her mum had called her midweek.

'No,' Susie said—and she was being honest. 'I've got a lot on my mind. I've been offered an apprenticeship.'

'Susie! That's fabulous. You won't have to do that expensive course in Florence.'

'I know.'

She looked at her new white uniform, hanging on the door; Pearla's had had her name embroidered on the jacket and Cucou had handed it to her yesterday.

No, Susie wasn't sulking—but she did have a lot on her mind.

When the call ended, she put down the phone and went to her bedside table to look at the result of her first ever pregnancy test.

Like Juliet, she'd decided it was time to face up to things.

INCINTA

She couldn't be pregnant.

But the pink word insisted she was.

'No...'

Susie shook her head and then checked the instructions again, told herself the test was surely wrong.

Because she was *not* going to be pregnant by some family law attorney who was too cynical for words and couldn't even commit to a week ahead, let alone a relationship.

She started to cry, and it was like a dam breaking.

She'd been on the edge of tears so many times, but now, as her entire world shifted, she broke down.

She lay on her bed and hugged her beautiful white jacket. She knew she'd have to say no to the apprenticeship.

And of course she'd have to tell Dante.

But how?

She would head back to England and deal with things there, she decided. Because, despite what she'd said to Dante that morning, she did not want to be the talk of this town.

Oh, and she would be. The two brothers couldn't even have a small scuffle on the walls without word getting out. Imagine the gossip about an apprentice chef at Pearla's being pregnant by Dante Casadio…

She didn't want it for herself, nor for Dante, nor Gio…

No, she didn't want her baby to be a piece of scandalous gossip.

Nor an accident.

She was certain that was what *she'd* been. And it told her what she didn't want for her own child.

She wanted to be a confident, loving mother.

Not one who resented giving up her fledgling career…

The tears stopped then, and there was a very wobbly sense of calm…

She'd be okay, Susie told herself.

Not for a second would she think of this as an accident.

Susie limped through the week on autopilot.

She even made a cake for her own birthday…

Susie
Happy 25th

'When's the party?' Louanna asked.

Juliet sat with a little frown between her green eyes, watching Susie piping hearts and flowers...

'Tomorrow,' Susie replied.

'Good, because we're both working tonight—it's the ball...'

Susie looked over to Juliet. 'Are you playing?'

'Yes!' She beamed, though her features were as white as marble. 'But only because the understudy broke her wrist.'

'You'll be perfect,' Susie assured her. 'Oh, I wish I was going.'

'Maybe next year,' Louanna said.

And the shaky sense of calm Susie was perched upon cracked a little as she glimpsed this time next year, and the whole live person she'd be responsible for.

There would be no ball next year, or the year after that, Susie decided, and messed up one of her pretty flowers.

And anyway, the only person she wanted to take her to the ball was Dante.

'Are you okay?' Juliet checked. 'Your icing...'

Yikes.

And then it dawned on her that there was no Prince Charming required when she had a fairy godmother.

She didn't need Dante to make her wishes come true.

And while she still had the chance, she was going to embrace everything!

Everything.

'Susie!' Mimi embraced her.

'Is it too late to say yes?' she asked.

'To what?'

'The ball.'

'The ball?' Gio called out. 'But it's tonight.'

'Don't listen to him,' Mimi said, and then she gave her a bright smile. 'Of course it's not too late.'

She invited her in while she collected her coat. Then, 'Gio, my love, Susie and I are going to my sister's for a few hours...'

Dante peered at his unshaven reflection in the mirror.

God, he looked like Gio in decline.

Or Gio in love.

It was late on Saturday afternoon and he picked up the phone to make the call he had to.

He knew he couldn't look to the future without clearing the past.

'Dante.' Sev was curt when he answered.

'Can we talk?'

'No. I don't have time. I'm trying to get to Lucca *again*, to attend the ball, because you couldn't be bothered to—'

'Sev,' Dante cut in, and he thought of Susie and those words that had stung. He refused to throw in the towel. 'I've met someone.'

'I have to board.' Sev was not giving an inch.

'Her name's Susie.'

'I know,' Sev said. 'The waitress.'

'How do you know?'

'I'm your brother, Dante.'

'For the first time since the accident there aren't awful memories on every corner in Lucca,' Dante said, thinking how when he thought of home now he could see Susie on the walls, or standing under an umbrella. And when he looked at the hills, instead of seeing twisted metal and a graveyard, he thought of her sitting on the couch at the winery. 'Can you get that?'

'I wish I could get that,' Sev said.

'Can we meet? Can we speak?'

'Tomorrow,' Sev said, 'but I don't want to drag up the past.'

'I don't see how we can move on if we don't.'

'I have to go; I really am boarding now...' Sev told him—and then he swore.

'What?'

'It's delayed. I'm going to try and sort out another flight.'

'Where are you?'

'Edinburgh.'

Dante looked at his new, or rather old, gold watch. 'You're not going to make it.'

'You'll have to go to the ball.'

He was going to hell, Dante knew as he packed his tux, because if Susie found out he was in Lucca and at the ball she would never forgive him.

He called her from the car on the way and got her voicemail.

'Look, I know it's too late to ask you to the ball, but I have to attend. So I'm going to be in Lucca tonight. I wondered if...' He grimaced. It sounded as if he wanted to drop by for a hook-up. 'Okay, scrap that. I'll call you as soon as I can.'

Right now, he had a lot to arrange...

'Oh, Susie...'

Mimi had performed utter magic.

The dress was still gorgeous, the softest grey with a blush of pink, and now she was squeezed into a pair of very beautiful shoes...

She could have looked by far too pale—especially as she was feeling a little peaky—but the make-up had transformed her.

Mimi had always done her own stage make-up, and now Susie stared in the mirror with eyes that were vivid and blue as she blinked her long lashes. Her lips were a very pale pink.

Her heavy curls had been smoothed, and loose curls fell down over one shoulder.

She wished things could be different, but accepted this was how they were.

She'd felt alone all her life.

Maybe it was time to embrace it. To accept it and simply enjoy it.

'You are going to be very popular,' Gio told her.

He'd arranged for a car to take her, and had taken a walk over to Mimi's sister's to wave Susie off and then take a nice early-evening stroll on the walls with his new wife.

'You can tell me how Dante's speech is received,' he said.

'Dante?' She frowned, certain that Gio had got it wrong. 'He's not going.'

'No, he's there. Sev won't be arriving until later. So there will be a Casadio there tonight after all.'

Her heart seemed to stop for a second, even two, and then it skipped into overdrive, her pulse racing in her temples.

Damn him...

She felt her newly painted nails digging into her palms, frustration and anger building at the fact that he'd do this again.

Surely he'd have called?

Then she checked her phone. And as it turned out he had...

He was in town and he was going to the ball. It would seem he was hoping to drop by.

God, he had a nerve!

'Thank you, Mimi,' she said as she climbed into the car, battling her feelings and trying not to let the happy couple see.

'Now, remember,' Mimi said, 'it's all about the entrance.'

'Yes.'

'You pause, and then you smile.' She looked right at Susie. 'You *smile*,' she said. 'Even if it kills you. Even if it is a hostile audience.'

'Got it.' Susie nodded.

It was a pink sky evening, just coming into spring, and the narrow cobbled streets were lined with impressive cars, filled with beautiful people.

Dante was going to be there...

The anger and hurt she'd been holding in was suddenly met with a surge of relief—like headwinds colliding on a clifftop. She felt battered. Surges of frustration met with the sheer relief that Dante would be there tonight.

And this, Susie decided, was how she wanted to face him. This would be his memory of her when she called him from England or they met to deal with legal papers.

Not pale and washed out outside her apartment after a double shift at the restaurant. Cross and pleading with him to take her to the ball.

She could do this by herself.

All of it.

She wanted him to know that.

The car arrived at the magnificent building, beautifully lit, and she saw beautiful women and elegant men milling on the stairs in the portico.

And now it was her turn to arrive.

The door was opened and a gloved hand was offered, and she stepped out of the vehicle onto a rich navy carpet.

She stood alone.

And it was then that she saw him.

He was standing by a pillar—not leaning on it as such, just with the edge of his shoulder touching it. He was looking impossibly gorgeous in a tux, and he didn't even glance in her direction at first—just cast a bored eye over the stunning surroundings and skimmed past her.

Then he frowned and turned around.

And she smiled. Not because Mimi had told her to, and

not to kill him or show him how brilliant her life was without him...

Simply, she was pleased to see him.

It was as if her lips hadn't caught up with her playing it cool, so it was an utterly natural smile, and it only wavered when he didn't smile back.

He just stared, and so did she, because...actually...he didn't look quite his usual self.

'*Signorina...*'

She was being called to smile for the cameras, and then she was ushered through a sea of people and colour and so much noise.

Glasses clinking...the hum of chatter...all spilling forward as she followed the music into the ballroom, where huge chandeliers spun beams of light.

She looked over to the orchestra. There was Juliet, her red hair glowing, her concentration fully on the music. But then she glanced over and gave her a gorgeous smile and a nod.

'You look stunning.'

She heard Dante's voice and turned slightly.

'Thank you.' She looked at him a little more closely. 'So do you.'

However, she looked at his unshaven jaw and was reminded of his comment about calling an ambulance if he ever went out unshaven.

But it was not her place to comment like that now.

She took a glass of champagne from a passing tray—then remembered she couldn't drink it. This pregnancy thing was all so new.

She stood awkwardly, holding her glass, and found that the thought of her baby was the one thing that didn't scare her tonight.

It was the thought of all the days when there would be no chance of seeing him.

Of lawyers and odd visits that Dante didn't even know about yet.

And she wouldn't be telling him here!

She kept her smile pasted on. 'Gio said you're making a speech?'

'A short one—unless Sev gets here in time...'

'He's coming too?'

'Yes.' He looked at her. 'I called him—tried to talk to him.'

'Oh?'

'He told me I lacked responsibility.'

'Did he?' Susie gave a little laugh. 'You don't.' Then her laugh changed. 'I got your message...'

'I apologise for that. It sounded tacky.'

'Just a bit.' Susie nodded.

'Would you like to dance?'

She wanted to say no—to be petty, to be bitter, and flounce off and dance with every other man in the room.

Only there wasn't a single man in the world she wanted to dance with more.

'That would be lovely.'

She had never danced to an orchestra, and she had never done any formal dancing—just watched it on the television. But either some of it had caught her attention or she had the perfect partner, because Dante made it smooth and easy, even when she faltered.

'Left...' he said, and then, 'Just one little step back...'

It was enough for her to dance without thought.

'I'm a fraud!' She smiled. 'I know only one dance step.'

'I don't think I'm thinking about your feet.'

'Please don't flirt.' She looked up at him.

'That's an impossible ask,' he told her.

But the compliments stopped, and they danced in silence, and she wished the music would never end.

For a while it didn't—but Dante was not here just for fun.

'I have to dance with a few guests,' he told her.

'Of course.'

'I don't want to.'

'Go.'

And it was fine being there alone. There were plenty of offers to dance, and gorgeous people to talk to, and even had Dante not been there it was something she wouldn't have missed for the world.

The tables were filled with scented blooms and gorgeous treats and she was *not* going home with Dante, Susie told herself.

Promised herself.

No matter how tempted, no matter how smooth his delivery, she would decline.

She would be leaving tonight in utter control.

'Scusi...' someone said, and she realised she was standing at one of the exits.

She moved a little closer to a table as the music was silenced and the speeches began.

There were a lot of thank-yous, and then an elderly, very distinguished-looking man took the microphone and spoke so fast that even with all her classes and language lessons she could barely understand what was being said.

'Sevandro Casadio...' the MC said, and then corrected himself. *'Scusi...* Dante Casadio...'

'Grazie...'

Dante thanked all the people who had already been thanked many times, and then he thanked Christos and his wife, saying that without their skill the wine would not be as rich. He thanked the orchestra, and then he spoke of how this night meant spring was here...all colour and beauty.

'My grandfather and his beautiful wife Mimi are delighted to support this night, loved by so many...' He slipped it in smoothly, and even if word had already spread like wildfire there were a couple of gasps of surprise and then applause. 'I haven't attended this ball for a very long time,' Dante said. 'And I know I have been absent too long.'

She'd been proud of how she'd mostly kept up with his speech, but then he said something she thought she didn't understand...or perhaps she was fighting not to cry.

'It is good to be here and to be home.'

He stepped down from the stage just as someone else knocked into her, and Susie realised she'd drifted towards the exit again.

She wasn't okay, Susie knew.

And she felt a tear splash down her cheek.

She didn't want to leave.

Ever.

She loved this man who was now talking to an elderly couple, who were congratulating him on his speech.

And then she saw him talking to Sev, and they didn't seem quite so hostile.

She felt another tear splash out, and quickly wiped it away with her thumb.

It was time to go, Susie decided.

But Dante caught her hand.

'Dance?'

One more...

His hand was close to the small of her back, the other was holding her hand, but they were too far apart. His cologne was light, heavenly...

'I just spoke to Cucou,' Dante said. 'He tells me I am dancing with his new apprentice.'

She gulped. 'I haven't accepted yet,' she said.

'Why wouldn't you accept? It's everything you wanted?'

'I'm not so sure,' she attempted, but her voiced faded. It was all too new and too raw to attempt to sound dismissive as she farewelled long held dreams and so she hurriedly changed the topic. 'I know this piece…' she said, referring to the music. 'Juliet stuffs it up every time.'

He smiled, and she looked up at his unshaven jaw. Dante was tense—perhaps because his brother had arrived.

He pulled her in a little closer and she rested her head on his chest, so she could peek at the orchestra. It would seem Juliet had nailed it.

'Perfect…' Susie smiled as the music soared.

'Yes,' Dante said. 'Perfect.'

And they were flirting with their bodies now.

His hand was a little firmer on her back, the other rested on her waist, and her hand, left to its own devices, was now on his chest.

'Susie,' he said, as the clock inched forward and the crowd on the dance floor thinned. 'When I called—'

'Please don't, Dante.'

'I didn't think to ask you to the ball tonight because—'

'Dante!' He'd said enough already. 'Please don't.' She pulled back. 'I'm going to go to the ladies' room.'

She did so, and she topped up her lipstick and looked at her glittering eyes, and his words stung.

I didn't think to ask you…'

Have some pride, Susie!

So instead of heading back to the gorgeous ballroom, because she knew where that would lead—straight to bed— she went down to the foyer and out through the arches to the grand steps.

'Running away?'

His voice was like a deft arrow and it halted her, but she didn't let it fell her. She just turned around and shrugged.

'No.' She shook her head. 'I'm just leaving the same way I arrived. Alone.' She looked at him then. 'I can't believe you didn't ask me.' He said nothing. 'You've ruined my night.'

'How?'

'I wanted one perfect night. A photo of us arriving together. One time. So I could look back and say, *Oh, that's the guy. And that was me.*'

'Susie, it is not ruined—'

'But it is.'

She stared at him and then the floodgates opened, after a lifetime of being not quite enough, not fitting in, not getting to shine...

'I wanted something just for me. For...'

Us.

She didn't say it; she clamped her mouth closed before uttering the forbidden word.

It was silly. There was nothing of *them*. It was just that if she was having a baby, and if they were going to be bound only by lawyers or whatever, she'd wanted one memory...

And it wasn't just about showing her family and sisters; it was so much more.

More than that...

To show their baby...

That's your father and me.

One photo before it all turned to bitter dust.

One magical night and he had ruined it.

'You didn't even *think* to ask me?'

She threw his words back at him and stood trembling with hurt as he came down the steps, all lithe and nonchalant.

'Susie, the ball was the last thing on my mind until you arrived. You turned my head,' he told her. 'When you got out of that car, I couldn't take my eyes from you.'

'Too late.' Her eyes were brimming.

'It's never too late.' He smiled at her anger. 'Come back to mine.'

'You've got a nerve...'

'I do,' he said.

And he kissed her right there under the lights, his jaw

rougher than she'd ever known it and his mouth hungry and skilled and utterly perfect, persuasive...

It was by far safer to kiss him than to speak. She might tell him she loved him...that they were having a baby. So much easier to sink into reckless kisses that made her forget all her problems, her every care swept away by the dark, passionate tide he created.

'Susie...' His mouth left hers and now he lifted her hair and kissed her neck, then her bare shoulder. 'Come home with me...'

Her stance was wavering. One more night...she reasoned.

And his kisses slowed a little, like turning down the gas, and he took her to a simmer.

She hated how they'd ended. It was her only regret in their turbulent time.

'You left your scarf...'

She laughed at this most illogical reason for returning to his house, but it was good enough for now. 'I did,' she agreed, and her eyes closed as he kissed her to confirm, and the bells chimed in agreement, sweeping in a new day.

Her birthday.

It was not as if a louse like him would remember, but for now it didn't matter—it was still the best birthday of her life.

'*Fai strada tu*, Dante!'

Susie told him to lead the way and, picking up her skirts with one hand, holding his with the other, they walked together through the cobbled streets.

'Your Italian is getting better every day,' he told her.

'Yes,' Susie said, tongue in cheek. 'We did terms of endearment this week.' She laughed to herself. 'Not that you'd know anything about them,' she added with a teasing twist. '*Ciccina.*'

'*Ciccino,*' he corrected. '*I* am the sweetheart.'

Oh, he was so far from sweet as he stopped their walk home to kiss her against a very cold wall.

'What else?' he asked as he kissed her shoulder.

'Cucciolo,' she said.

She'd called him a puppy—a very affectionate term, but certainly not one that described Dante.

And then they made it to the gorgeous avenue and inside his door.

'Come,' he said, leading her towards the dining room. 'We can dance here as we wanted to.'

'I don't want to dance any more,' Susie said.

Her voice sounded unfamiliar, as if there was a new tone, one that had her shivering, and clearly it caused a reaction in him, for his hand halted as he pushed down the ornate handle. The dining door remaining closed as he stood utterly still.

'Dance?' he suggested again, and his voice was low too, husky.

He cleared his throat and turned around.

'I really don't want to,' she said.

Then he met her eyes, and perhaps saw the fire that was blazing there. There was no time for dancing.

'Oh, you know how to ruin plans,' Dante told her as he scooped her up in his arms.

'So do you,' Susie said, putting her hands around his neck.

She only let go when he dropped her on the bed.

She lay in a cloud of pink and grey and closed her eyes as he lifted the hem of the gown to reveal the pale pink flesh of her thighs, and then impatiently he moved the material higher, up to her stomach.

'Careful,' she warned. 'It's not my gown.'

'Shh,' he told her.

And although it was clear he'd wanted them downstairs, in the firelit dining room, instead here they were—upstairs, the bed turned back, the mattress plump and waiting...

He pulled down her lacy knickers and she lost a shoe as he pushed them past her ankles…

'Oh, Susie…' he said, in that low, seductive voice, and he lowered his lips to the soft flesh of her stomach.

And when he spoke her name like that she had no choice but to close her eyes…to feel adored and wanted, even if it could not last.

'What else did you learn to say?' he asked with desire in his eyes, as if goading her to tell him how she really felt.

'I can't remember,' Susie said, terrified that she might say something she'd later regret.

'What else?' he persisted, and his hot mouth moved down her stomach.

He stroked her, his eyes moving down, and as he found her tenderest spot she felt tight inside, tight with desire as his fingers slipped inside her. She bit down on her bottom lip as he explored her—and then he looked up and met her eyes.

'*Settemila baci per te,*' Dante said. 'Did you learn that?'

'No…' Although she sort of understood what he'd said. But she didn't really have the capacity to play the game right now, so she shook her head.

'It means,' Dante told her, 'seven thousand kisses to you.'

He lowered his head and delivered several of them.

How did he make this so easy?

He simply did. Because she parted so easily, and as his soft mouth caressed her, as he explored her so exquisitely, her homework continued. But it was in breathless attempts at words rather than practice phrases.

'*Mi piace*…it's nice,' she told him. '*Mi piace…*' she said again. Only her voice was more urgent now, and it told him it was specifically there that he pleased her. Then she told him what he had once said to her, and it came from a very natural place. '*Non ti fermare!*'

Don't stop!

He was so intense, so specific with his mouth, and he did not stop. Even as her hips lifted his mouth chased them. And then she gave up on their game, because she did not trust the words that might slip out as he took her to bliss.

How many kisses it took, she lost count. She felt as if she were floating, almost aching for him to take her, to make love to her, to fill her. And yet she never wanted it to end. Her hands were knotted in his thick black hair, and his delivery so honed she fought not to push him away, because she wanted it so.

It didn't take seven thousand kisses.

She climaxed under his skilful mouth and sobbed out words in a language she didn't know as she simply gave in...

She was trying to breathe, hoping she hadn't told him she loved him, but Dante wasn't listening anyway.

Unbelted and unzipped, he took her.

'There,' he told her, and she was on fire, clinging to the sheets.

He was holding her hips. And she was spent, yes, but still being ravished, watching him through her half-closed eyes and adoring him.

Because she did adore him.

He climaxed with a hollow shout, and it felt as if the air he breathed out stroked her inside, and she found there was a little left to give as she orgasmed again to the last thrusts of him.

'I can't breathe...' she told him.

'You are,' he said.

And he turned her around on the bed and undid her gown. And she lay there, watching him undress. Then he dealt with the rest of her clothes, and with a few deft movements from Dante...

She was back in his bed.

CHAPTER ELEVEN

SHE HAD ALWAYS loved their mornings.

'Morning,' he said, stroking her spine, and she turned and smiled right into his eyes.

And even if she was unsure of what lay ahead, waking to Dante would always be perfect.

'You look like a panda,' he told her.

'I'm sure that I do.'

They just lay together and stared, and she didn't quite know what to say.

It was Dante who spoke. 'I didn't think to ask you to the ball, because for me the ball is a duty. Yesterday it was the furthest thing from my mind.' He sat up in the bed. 'I'll get coffee.'

'Tea for me.'

'Tea?' He frowned. 'Do you want some breakfast?'

'No, thanks.' Susie grimaced at the very thought, then saw him frown again. 'Too much champagne,' she said.

Dante nodded and picked up a towel. She lay back in his sumptuous bed, wondering how she could bear to leave, and how she could possibly stay.

Susie knew she was running away—but she didn't want to see the disappointment in his eyes. She wanted him to find out from a distance...

Tea? Dante raided his cupboards, but there was no tea to be had.

Then he went into the dining room to collect a certain box,

and saw the champagne that had been cooling there floating in a bucket of water.

Susie hadn't even had a sip of champagne last night.

And she hadn't yet said yes to an apprenticeship at Pearla's, when it was everything she wanted.

Dante wasn't a top attorney for nothing.

She was pregnant.

He waited for the punch in his guts, only it never came. But he did sit down at the dining room table for some time.

He rather guessed she didn't want to have the baby here. If he was her attorney, he'd advise her to be on a flight back to England straight away.

Susie was possibly leaving. With his baby. But instead of being angry he didn't blame her.

Had she known when he'd told her about what had happened with Rosa?

Dante put his head in his hands, thinking of their row after the wedding and all he'd said…

A baby.

Why was he just sitting there when he should be pacing?

Why wasn't he panicking that it was too soon or pounding up the stairs?

A baby…

He kept going back to that…picturing something he'd never imagined for himself. A daughter or a son…

After so much pain and grief, the thought of Susie having his baby felt like a rusty knife being pulled from his chest.

But before all that he had to know Susie's thoughts.

Dante knew his.

But they both had to speak the truth.

The tea took quite a long time coming—in fact she was half dozing when the bedroom door was pushed open.

'Happy Birthday to You…'

She started as a gorgeous Dante, who could actually sing, pushed aside his embarrassment, and she simply bathed in the glow as he came in carrying a tray. She sat up, stunned to see there was even a little cake, with a candle lit.

'You remembered.'

'Well, it's not like you let me forget,' he pointed out. 'A seven-year-old would be less excited.'

She let out a gurgle of laughter, then sighed in delight when she saw the beautiful cake, her name piped in pink with little silver hearts, and knew it was Cucou's work.

'It's wonderful...'

'Blow,' Dante said. 'I want some cake. It's your favourite,' he added.

'How do you know?'

'I asked the pastry chef. Raspberry, with liqueur and cream and white chocolate...'

He was slicing away and it was her first proper cake of her own.

Her favourite cake had his bed feeling like a little boat in an ocean storm.

'I might save it for later. Have a huge slice then...'

'Too much champagne?' He put the knife down. 'You won, by the way.'

'Won what?'

'Whatever this competition is with your sisters. They will be very jealous,' he said as he handed her his phone. 'You look stunning.'

'Gosh!' She looked at the picture of herself arriving at the ball and instead of feeling sad, felt proud to have gone alone. 'Go, me!'

'There are a few.' He scrolled through them. 'A back shot... Look at that poor guy on the stairs. Homeless from the neck up, as Gio would say.'

She laughed when she saw he was referring to himself.

And she had her photo. Dante was gazing at her, and she at him.

That's your father and me.

Yes, she had her photo.

She looked up. Did she dare tell him now? Shatter this perfect morning?

No, she decided, because that was for later. This morning was simply about her and Dante. The morning he'd brought her a cake and made it the best birthday ever.

'Here,' he said, and handed her a parcel.

It was wrapped in gold paper and there was even a wax seal, and a slender golden rope.

'It's beautiful…'

'I think you have to open it to say that.' Then he looked at her as a tear slid down her cheek. 'Why are you crying?'

'Is this from your PA? The bauble that ends it all?'

'No.' His voice was suddenly serious. 'This is from me. And I admit I'm nervous.'

'Why?'

'I have never bought a birthday gift before.'

'Never?'

'Not for a long time. Maybe a bottle of whisky for Gio. We don't really…' He fell into a silence that said more than words—for him, birthdays and family celebrations had stopped a long time ago. 'Hopefully you'll like it.'

He might not have wrapped it personally, but Dante had definitely written the little card attached.

Tutti bella.
Dante

Everything beautiful.

No kiss by his name, and yet her heart was thumping even before she'd peeled off the paper. She already loved it!

The box was walnut and gleaming, and when she opened it up Susie gasped. It was a circle of jewelled flowers, nestled in velvet. Then she saw that it was actually a necklace—and not just any necklace, nor just any flowers.

'Magnolias…' she breathed.

There were so many stones and different precious metals, swirls of enamel. Everywhere she looked she saw more. Pale sapphires, pink rubies and little emeralds, seed pearls and delicate flowers.

'Magnolias…' she said again. 'It's perfect. Where on earth did you find this?'

'Locally,' Dante told her, and took it out of the box. 'Let me put it on you.'

'I want to see it…'

He wasn't listening, so she lifted her hair, and he fiddled with the clasp, and then he took a hand mirror from beside the bed.

'I have never seen anything so heavenly…'

'I should have given it to you last night.'

'No.' She shook her head. 'It's perfect for my birthday.'

She started to cry, her panda eyes spreading, and kept peeling tissues from the box he handed to her.

'Thank you.'

'You're very welcome.' Then he looked at her. 'And a good choice, given you won't be here for the magnolias.'

She went still.

'You're going back to England.'

'I never said that…'

'Aren't you?' Dante asked. 'Can't we both speak the truth?'

She swallowed.

'Susie, I wouldn't want to tell me either.'

Her eyes darted up.

'But can I tell you one thing? I know I seem ruthless, but I'm not to the people I care about.'

'Dante…' She was shaking a little, still unsure what he knew.

'Incinta?' he asked—pregnant.

'I'm late…'

'The truth, Susie.'

'I *am* late.'

'You don't have to break it to me gently,' he said. 'I think I already know. And I don't think you'd be talking about throwing in your dream job if you hadn't taken a test, and you didn't drink any champagne last night. You don't want cake now.'

'Yes,' she finally said. 'I am.'

'When did you find out?'

'I think I was starting to work it out at the wedding.'

'Poor thing!'

He actually laughed, just a little, and it was so unexpected—more so the hand that came to her cheek.

'I did a test on Wednesday,' she said.

'So, when were you going to tell me?'

'Once I got home.'

He removed his hand.

'I didn't want an argument, or for you to…' She shrugged. 'Do your attorney thing and make the DNA speech.'

'I was nineteen when that happened,' Dante said.

'I get that.'

'Do you want to go it alone?' he asked. 'Seriously, Susie? I *am* an attorney, but I am not going to plead for marriage or for you to stay here. I am going to do my best, whatever you want…' Then he added, 'I'll be around, though. For the baby. A lot.'

She looked down.

'Well, depending on work,' he amended, and she smiled just a little.

She looked up and met his eyes for the first time since she'd nodded and confirmed that, yes, she was pregnant.

'So, what do you want?' he asked.

'There'll be a lot of gossip if I'm here.'

'There's gossip now.' Dante shrugged. 'Susie, please tell me what you want, or what you think you want, or *something*?'

She was scared to, though.

'Okay,' he said into the silence. 'Shall I tell you what I would prefer?'

'Yes.'

'Marriage,' he said.

'Don't say that.'

'I am saying that,' Dante told her. 'That's what I want. Okay, I'll tell you my ideal and then you can tell me what you want.'

'We don't know each other,' she argued. 'We only met a few weeks ago, and you've been in Milan most of the time.'

'And miserable without you.'

'My God…' She looked at him then, her eyes angry. 'You couldn't even commit to a ball, you didn't even invite me last night, and now you tell me you want marriage?'

'I love you.'

'Okay,' she amended. 'Now you tell me that you love me and want to marry me.'

'I do.' He nodded. 'I've told you what I want—it's your turn now.'

'A pause,' Susie said. 'To let the news sink in and so you can get used to the idea.'

There was more silence, and then he arrogantly broke it. 'That's your pause—I'm used to it now.'

'You can't be…'

'Are you?'

'No!' she shouted, and then she heard her own voice and heard her lie. 'Yes…' She was bewildered. 'I'm not Zen with it, or anything, but…'

'Let's talk about us,' he suggested. 'The baby's fine—we'll work it out. What about us?'

It wasn't the baby that was the issue now. He would take

care of their child, however she wanted to play it, and she loved him for that.

She loved him.

Susie looked at the man she loved, at his chocolate-brown eyes and his unshaven jaw, and she didn't want him *trying* to build a future with her just because he felt it was the right thing to do.

'I think it's too soon for it to be love,' she told him.

'So you want to wait? See what happens? How you feel in a few months? How I feel is not going to change.'

'I don't believe you love me, Dante. I think you're trying to do the right thing...make up for what happened with Rosa.'

'Do not bring her into our bed.'

'Or you're trying to make Gio happy.'

'Do you know what I do for work? I sit with men and women who have married for the wrong reasons, or stayed together for the wrong reasons, or who are breaking up for the wrong reasons. I am not going to lie about love.'

'So when did you decide you loved me?'

'You're annoying me now,' Dante told her. 'I'm the one looking like a fool here. I just told you I love you. Now, if you don't love me, say so. I can take it.'

'I do love you.'

'Good!' he said. 'When did you know that?'

Susie thought back, and it was a hard thing to pinpoint... Given their short time frame, she could hardly say it had crept up on her.

'Always,' she admitted. 'I didn't realise it, but...' She nodded. 'Always.' Then she thought that might be a bit much. 'Maybe a couple of days in.'

'Well, I don't know quite when it happened for me, but...'

'Please don't say it if you don't mean it.'

'I promise you I would not. I called our jeweller and asked for the necklace to be made on my first day back at work.'

Susie frowned.

'I think I got cold feet,' he went on. 'And then he sent the designs.'

'You had this made?'

'I did.' He nodded. 'It was to be a farewell gift; I was never going to tell you it had been designed with you in mind. That felt like a bit much. So yes, maybe I did get cold feet.'

She reached up and struggled to take it off, just to take another, better look. Dante knelt up in the bed and helped her.

'I heard you wanted something chosen specifically for you...your little jealousy issue.'

And then he made her smile and he made her cry as he talked her through the stones.

'Pale sapphire—that dress you wore. I was like a fifteen-year-old... I told myself it was just sex.' He pointed to the darker sapphires. 'Your eyes.' Then to the little collection of tiny diamonds. 'The bubbles in the sink at Gio's...'

Her breath grew shallow as he took her through their time together.

'The pink and lilac I left to the jeweller, and the grass is enamel, I think, maybe with little gems?'

'Is it a tiny ladybird...?'

'No,' he said. 'That was a late addition this Wednesday. I had the ruby flown to Signor Adino.'

The air went still.

'I know you wanted fresh stones, and new metals, but I have never known what to do with the rubies. One for Sev...one for me. I wanted something nice for it.' He thought for a moment. 'Yes, I guess I officially knew I loved you on Wednesday.'

Susie turned and kissed him. It was a kiss that wasn't anything other than a loving kiss, a blissful one, and the bed was still and steady now, all nerves gone.

'Marry me,' he said. 'Up in the hills. Because when I think of them now, I think of you.'

'Marry me,' Susie said. 'I get to ask,' she told him, 'because I loved you first.' She smiled.

'Well, I'm not so sure about that…'

It was a delicious debate to have.

EPILOGUE

SUSIE WAS FINALLY the talk of the town—and was very happy to be.

She'd arrived in December, was marrying in May... And, yes, there had been a lot of nudges as the restaurant's patrons peered into the kitchen at the new apprentice chef who was dating Dante...and possibly showing her pregnancy a little.

Now, on her wedding day, her little bump was irrefutable.

Her dress was a simple one—white, but with the tiniest hint of pink, and only if the light was right. It tied under her bust and flowed down to her pretty jewelled sandals. It was floaty and summery and perfect for a wedding at a winery in the lush Tuscan hills.

She held sunflowers, because they made everyone happy, and that was the only requisite on this gorgeous sunny day.

Oh, and she wore her necklace.

Susie hadn't wanted an engagement ring, and neither would she require an eternity ring. Even if not another soul ever knew that the so-called ladybird she wore on the necklace around her neck meant everything.

She could hear gorgeous music and, looking out, saw their guests. There was Juliet, her red hair stunning in the morning sun. And Louanna. She could make out Cucou and Pedro too.

Gio was seated with Mimi, but Mimi rose now, ready to perform and sing Susie up to the arch of flowers.

And then she saw Dante and Sev, walking together, and her heart swelled at the sight of the two brothers. Things were still very difficult between them—and, no, that particular conversation was yet to be had.

If ever.

For today, though, it was all pushed aside and they were brothers again.

'Okay,' her dad said as his phone bleeped. 'It's time.'

And so it was.

They walked down through the winery's restaurant and then out towards the vines, and it was stunning. Lavender and sunflowers waved in the distance, and the hills that had taken so much from this family seemed to be trying to make up for it today, for they were vivid with colour.

She could hear the wonderful string quartet, and she looked at the two brothers.

Mimi gestured to the bride to proceed, and then smiled at the groom and sang directly to him, telling Dante, in song, that his bride was approaching.

And as Mimi's glorious voice rose skywards something beautiful happened.

Both brothers looked down to their shoes, and then they turned to each other and shared a very tiny smile.

Then Dante turned and looked at his bride.

Susie was crying before she was halfway down the aisle, and although Dante didn't quite kiss the bride on her arrival, he embraced her.

'It's all good,' he told her.

And he looked down at her dress, took her flowers and handed them to one of the twins—he really didn't notice which one. The best man handed him a handkerchief and he dried

Susie's eyes, but when Dante touched the little ladybird on her necklace they filled again.

'For eternity,' he told her.

'Yes.'

Both knew how precious this love was.

* * * * *

MODERN

Glamour. Power. Passion.

Available Next Month

Carrying A Sicilian Secret Caitlin Crews

His Enemy's Italian Surrender Sharon Kendrick

On His Bride's Terms Abby Green

Engaged In Deception Kim Lawrence

Boss's Heir Demand Jackie Ashenden

Accidental One-Night Baby Julia James

Royal Fiancée Required Kali Anthony

After-Hours Proposal Trish Morey

Amore
Billion-Dollar Invitation Michele Renae
Fling With Her Boss Karin Baine